HEXES AND HEADLINES

A RAVENS HOLLOW INVESTIGATION
BOOK TWO

ELLA STONE

PAPER CAT PUBLISHING

Also by Ella Stone

The Dark Creatures Saga

Dark Creatures

Dark Destiny

Dark Deception

Dark Redemption

Dark Reckoning

The Bloodsuckers Blog Trilogy

Life Sucks

Love Bites

Lost Souls

The Ravens Hollow Investigations

Bylines and Bloodsuckers

Fangs and Front Pages

Hexes and Headlines

Demons and Deadlines

Curses and Copy

Nymphs an Newsreels

Sirens and Sources

BY ELLA STONE & HEATHER G. HARRIS

The Witchlight Magical Mysteries

Secrets of the Frostbound Cottage

Secrets of the Forgotten Heir

Secrets of the Deadly Nightshades

Secrets of the Eternal Flame

Secrets of the Hidden Heritage

Secrets of the Silenced Society

Text copyright © 2025 Ella Stone

Paper Cat Publishing

ISBN: 978-1-915346-58-2

Edited by Dayna Hart
Cover by Christian Bentulan

CHAPTER
ONE

Bunny Bandit.
Jewellery thief turns out to be the
family pet.

I stared at the title of my current article, not sure if I should laugh or cry. Over the course of the day, I had interviewed the family in question, watched on as Diego took photographs of said rabbit, and written a four hundred word piece on the light-fingered floof, who'd been stealing things from its owner and taking them back to their hutch. To be fair, it wasn't a bad article. It was heartfelt and humorous, not to mention packed full of details, from the dates the owners had first reported items going missing to the police, to the neighbours they'd fallen out with over the suspected thievery. Neighbours who were all too happy to pose for photos and insist that it was all water under the bridge.

In terms of the type of easy-reading fluff piece people

wanted to find in a small island paper, it was bang on the mark. Only I hadn't spent years working up the career ladder to write fluff pieces. I was an investigative journalist. Or at least I had been, before one of those investigations led to me losing my pulse and being thrown into the paranormal world. Now I was a vampire, living on the other side of the world, writing stories about thieving rabbits.

In fairness, my move to Ravens Hollow had meant to be a chance to slow down. To get used to this new version of me. Not to mention the island and town that I had moved to. But that plan of a quiet pace had been derailed when, on my very first night here just under two months ago, there'd been a murder at the annual art festival. As the police struggled to work out who was responsible for the gruesome death, it had been all hands on deck. Well, that's what I'd decided, anyway. I'm sure my new boss, Bobby, the editor-in-chief of the Ravens Hollow Oracle would've liked it if I'd slowed down a bit and taken my time settling into the paranormal community, rather than turning up on their doorsteps with a series of probing questions. Especially given how new a vampire I was – still am, for that matter – and how little I knew about the para world by then.

However, if I *had* slowed down and taken a backseat to the story, I wouldn't have uncovered the illegal egg smuggling operation happening right under our noses. And it wasn't chicken eggs we were talking about. No, these were paranormal creatures. Basilisks, Hydras. The report we got from the police even said there was a hippogryph egg in the mix. So... yeah. That had been one heck of an introduction into paranormal life. Thankfully, the people involved had been arrested – those who weren't killed by the creatures, that is – and operations shut down. After that, it was time to start enjoying normal life as a Ravens Hollow resident. Or as normal as it could be when your neighbours were a pixie and a poltergeist.

Three months ago, I would have thought anyone who said something like that was clearly taking something, but I genuinely was neighbours with a pixie, who loved gardening almost as much as they loved playing the piccolo, and a poltergeist who threw things at said pixie whenever they'd had enough of the music. I had to admit I was grateful for the interventions, given that it meant I didn't have to complain myself and would normally get a few nights' peace and quiet afterwards. Not that my house was completely quiet. Not with all the training I was doing with Pongo.

Still, other than the nighttime serenades and time spent walking and training Pongo, life was incredibly slow. Which I loved. But I was missing the rush that came with a decent story to investigate.

The bunny bandit fluff piece was pretty much on par with everything else I'd written over the last eight weeks, which included a write-up on a group of non-shifter seagulls that got drunk on an open bottle of mango hooch – the island's favourite tipple – and an extended piece on a red-panda-shifter who was using her own fur to make clothes. I never thought being a vampire could be dull. And yet, here I was, wishing something would happen.

The only thing that was worth any of my time were the hunting restrictions that had been placed on the island. Despite there being a total of five werewolf packs and various carnivorous shifters who called Ravens Hollow and the surrounding land home, they had been reduced to hunting in only sixty percent of the forests. While the mayor and the council maintained it was in the best interests of all the inhabitants, many residents disagreed, insisting it was actually putting the biodiversity of the landscape at risk. Two such residents were Ines Ortega and her sister Sofia.

I was working with Ines to get the story the attention it deserved, but it was difficult. The matter had been brought to the attention of the council almost a month ago, and they had yet to come back with any solutions.

As I stared at the computer, I let out a long sigh, then opened up an email, ready to ping the article across to Theodora, the copy editor.

Snack. Snack. Snack.

The single word echoed up from the floor by my feet.

I looked down. Pongo – the stray puppy I'd found when I first moved to Ravens Hollow – was aggressively hitting one of his multiple buttons sprawled out beneath my desk. Button-training Pongo was a work in process, and though we were now up to over a dozen individual words, occasionally he'd hit the wrong one and had to correct himself. But the way he continued to thump on the piece of plastic, he knew exactly what he wanted.

Snack. Snack.

'Don't worry, Pongo. I've got some,' Chloe said. My work bestie focused mainly on sports and events on the island and had a desk opposite from mine. 'Come here, boy.'

When I first arrived, the fae's hair had been a delicate lilac, but now it was a hot pink. She looked equally great in both.

'You should probably give him a couple,' I said as Pongo trotted over to her. She grabbed the jar of dog treats – which were even more expensive than the ones I got him – and unscrewed the lid. 'He always wants more than one.'

'I'm not surprised,' Chloe replied, dropping a few by his feet. 'I can't believe how much he's grown in the last few weeks. Do you know what breed he is yet?'

I bit down on my bottom lip, not really wanting to answer.

When I'd first found Pongo, he'd been a skinny ball of matted fur, and obviously I'd expected him to fill out and get bigger, just not at the rate he'd been doing so.

He was now at least double the size he had been. And with his mix of dark and light brown markings, my research had been annoyingly conclusive. As much as I didn't want to admit it, I was fairly sure I'd gotten myself a Leonberger.

Before Pongo I'd never even heard of the breed. Now though, I knew more than I wanted to. Like the fact they could grow up to 170lbs. Which meant that even though he was already bigger than the average springer spaniel,

he had a lot of growing left to do. He was already deci-
mating my food budget, which I could deal with, but a
more major issue was that I drove a Mini. A vintage Mini.
The type where anyone over five foot seven struggled to
even get inside. If he kept growing, the only way he'd fit
in the car would be with the window wound down and
his head hanging out. Fingers crossed we had a long time
until he got there.

'Oh, I'm sure he's just some kind of mixed breed,' I
said, flashing Chloe a hopeful smile.

A moment later, the speaker buzzed again.

Thank you, it said. Chloe beamed.

'You're welcome, Pongo,' she said, her smile growing
wider still. 'You're such a polite boy, aren't you?'

She slipped another biscuit out of the jar and handed
it to him, carefully avoiding my gaze, as if I wouldn't
notice.

'Those buttons are such a good idea,' she said. 'I can't
believe how easily he can communicate with them.'

'I agree,' I said. 'The only problem is, now he wants to
bring them everywhere with us.'

'Well, that's a good thing, isn't it? Means you can
always know what he's thinking.'

'True, I suppose.'

Dog training had started in earnest after I'd recov-
ered from a nasty mermaid venom sting. Mermaid
venom. I wouldn't have believed it was an actual thing if
I hadn't experienced the agony myself. But hey, I had the
scar to prove it. A very thin hairline scar that ran along
my forearm. Considering I'm immortal, I assumed it

would have disappeared, but it had turned a soft silver, and I had the feeling it was going to be with me for life. However long that was.

Pongo wasn't to blame for me getting cut. The venomous scratch came courtesy of the former head of the mermaid mafia. But Pongo had turned up at the scene, desperate to help and protect me and that was something he just couldn't do. Firstly, because he was a pup, but also because he wasn't the best at listening or follow instructions. Even getting him to sit had been a trial. So, we'd started button training. So he could tell me exactly what he wanted.

It had its advantages. But I wouldn't say it was without problems either.

Bored. The word buzzed up from the floor. *Walk. Bored. Walk. Bored. Bored.*

'You and me both, buddy,' Diego said, strolling across from his desk on the other side of the office. 'It's a bit slow here, isn't it? Don't worry – you'll get used to it.'

'Believe it or not,' came another voice from across the office, 'some of us do still have plenty of work to do. So it'd be great if you could keep the noise down. I need to get these copy edits done before we go to print.'

'Sorry, Theodora,' the three of us chorused.

The Ravens Hollow Oracle was a lot smaller than the paper I'd worked at in London. Just six of us in total. Initially, I'd assumed I'd find it claustrophobic, working so closely with such a small team, but the truth was, they were great. Even Theodora, when she wasn't on deadline.

'Speaking of work...' Dylan said, coming over to join the three of us. 'I need to speak to some advertisers. Thought I might as well make the most of the sun and take the call at the beach bar. Fancy coming, Chloe?'

Whilst I knew what type of paras both Chloe and Diego were, I had yet to figure out what sect Dylan and Theodora belonged to. One thing I had figured, however, was that Dylan was hopelessly in love with Chloe. But she was engaged to Mick, a man I had never met, but who was known island wide, first for running the only auto shop on the island, and secondly for being co-brewer of the famous mango hooch.

'Sounds great,' Chloe said. 'Only there's the wolf pack lacrosse tournament in Wraith Woods this afternoon. I'm going to head over there in five.'

'Next time then.'

'Of course,' she said, flashing him a smile that I, and everyone else in the office, could see made him melt.

'I'll hold you to that,' He grinned as he picked up his satchel and headed over to the door, before pressing his foot down on Pongo's button.

Bye, the speaker chirped.

'Bye, Dylan,' we replied in unison.

As the door clicked shut behind him, Diego leaned closer to me.

'Have you been listening in to what's going on in there?' he said, nodding his head towards Bobby's office.

I'd more or less got to grips with my vampire senses now, including tuning in and out of different noises at will, instead of just whenever my body decided I should.

Like me, Diego's hearing was well beyond that of a tip, and most paras too, meaning we could both listen into conversations going on behind closed doors if we wanted to.

But Bobby was my boss, and a good one. That wasn't something I was okay doing.

'No,' I shook my head. 'Have you?'

'No,' Diego replied, his eyes still trained on the door. 'It's weird, though. Bobby never has his door shut like that. But this is the third time this week. Maybe we should, just to see if he's okay?'

'What are you whispering about?' Chloe said, her eyes narrowing on us. 'You know, it's really rude.'

'Sorry, you're right,' I said, not even sure why Diego and I had been whispering, anyway. It wasn't like Bobby would be able to hear us from inside of his office. 'We were just talking about Bobby.'

'Bobby?' Theodora said as she swivelled to face us. Apparently, she'd not been quite as focused on her work as she'd pretended. 'What were you saying?'

Diego and I looked at each other, mostly to decide which one of us was going to speak. There was no point hiding the truth from Theodora. As far as I was aware, she'd been working at The Oracle almost as long as Bobby, and if anyone was likely to know what was up with him, it would be her. But before either of us could say another word, Bobby's voice bellowed from his office.

'Just give it up! No, you listen to me. You call me one more time, and I'm calling the police. This ends now.'

TWO

There was no need for vampire hearing to catch what Bobby had just said or the tone in which he'd said it. Although my extra hearing did allow me insight into how he slammed the phone down on his desk so heavily the entire table had shaken. I wouldn't have been surprised if he'd broken one of the legs. Or cracked the top. Bobby was a big man.

'Well... that doesn't sound good,' Chloe whispered, worry clouding her face. 'Do you think he's alright?'

'Obviously not,' Diego replied. 'Think we should go in? See if we can do anything?'

It was the same thought I was having, though Theodora was the one who answered as she finally gave up doing her copy-editing and joined us gathered around my desk.

'If Bobby wants to talk, he'll talk to us,' she said firmly.

Bobby, the button buzzed. *Sad. Bobby sad.*

While the others' attention was still locked on Bobby's door, I looked at Pongo in disbelief. The sad button had been added to his vocab repertoire to help him understand the feeling that he felt when he was told he couldn't have any more snacks, or when I couldn't take him for a walk the instant he decided he wanted to go. He'd never used it in conjunction with someone else before.

'Clever boy, Pongo,' I said, grabbing one of the treats I kept in my top drawer and giving it to him. 'I think you're right. I think Bobby is sad.'

'Maybe,' Chloe said. 'Though he sounded more angry to me.' Silence swelled around us. I could tell that like me, Diego wanted to check on Bobby, but Theodora had said to leave it, and as difficult as I found it, it was probably worth listening to her.

'Well, I should probably go,' Chloe said, breaking the silence as she stood up. 'This lacrosse match won't wait for me.' She had grabbed her coat from the back of her chair and slung her bag over her shoulder when Bobby's door swung open. 'Or... I could just wait,' she whispered and hastily let go of the coat before slipping back into her seat.

'You need to ask him what's going on,' Diego whispered as Bobby marched into the kitchenette.

'Why can't you?' I hissed back.

'It'll look odd if I come across as caring,' he said. 'That's not my style.' He pulled a chocolate bar out of his pocket and tore open the wrapper casually.

'Is one of you going to ask what happened?' Chloe

joined in, though she wasn't quite as skilled at the whispering as Diego and me, and Pongo tilted his head curiously.

I could hear Bobby in the kitchenette, filling the kettle with water. I hadn't known it was possible to do such an ordinary act in an aggressive manner, but somehow he was managing. His pulse was still elevated, and even if I wasn't finely attuned to all the nuances of human scent, I could sense how high his stress was.

'Fine,' I muttered, rolling my eyes so that Chloe could see my response too. 'I'll go.'

With no idea what I was going to say, I ambled across to the kitchenette, casting several glances over my shoulder as I went, just in case one of the others decided they wanted to come and offer me some support. Though when I reached the door and found myself staring at Bobby's back I was still very much on my own. After a slight breath in, I cleared my throat, announcing my presence.

'You know... sometimes talking about it helps,' I offered gently. 'You sounded a little... agitated in there.'

'Agitated?' Bobby twisted around to face me. As always, he wore an oversized eyepatch over the right side of his face, which covered part of his left eye. Still, what was visible of it flashed with anger as his jaw was so tightly clenched I was surprised he hadn't cracked a molar. 'No, Elodie, I'm not agitated. I'm pissed at people who can't take no for an answer.'

'Any people specifically?'

He let out a sigh. 'Specifically, people from the mainland, trying to get in here and buy the paper.'

A gasp echoed out from the office behind me, and I spun around to find the other three staring at us, jaws open. To give them their dues, they didn't even pretend not to be listening.

'No... they aren't,' Chloe's voice trembled. 'They can't.'

'They are,' Bobby replied flatly. 'The Cali Chronicle. They've been sniffing around for years. Got a new guy in now, though. Aggressive. Thinks if he pesters me enough, I'll give in just to shut him up. Don't know me at all, if that's what he thinks.'

'How long have you had the Oracle?' I asked. I wasn't sure if it was something the others knew, but it was a question I'd wondered for a long time, and despite the current situation, now finally felt like an appropriate time to ask.

'Oh... must be coming up to eighty years now.'

'Eighty?' I coughed.

Sure, Bobby didn't look young, and that skewed eyepatch was just about hiding what type of para he truly was, but I was pretty certain it was one of a mythical origin. But did being mythical mean he lived longer than, say, a werewolf? Surely it didn't make him immortal like I was? I'd pegged him as somewhere in his late sixties, but clearly that estimate was way off. What did that mean? Was he still going to be here in a century's time, writing articles about crocheting centaurs and tap-dancing tree elves while throwing in the occasional investigative piece? It certainly felt like it.

Not that I knew if either of those creatures actually existed. But given I'd already come face-to-face with a real-life basilisk, and warded against the lure of an immortal, cursed male siren, I figured just about anything was possible.

'So, what are you going to do?' Diego's voice broke the silence. 'About this Chronicle guy?'

'Nothing,' Bobby said. 'Nothing to be done about him. Just wait it out until he goes away. It's the pestering that drives me nuts. I mean, how the hell he has time to call me up day and night, while supposedly running his own paper, beats me. Now—' He looked around the room and frowned, like he'd only just noticed us. 'What are we all doing, gassing? I've got a paper to keep running, you know.'

'I'm working,' Theodora said. She had somehow slipped back to her desk like she hadn't just been listening in on the entirety of that conversation.

'I was about to go and report on the lacrosse tournament,' Chloe said, glancing at her watch only for a wave of panic to cross her face. 'Man, I should have already left!'

She snatched up her coat, offered Pongo a quick ruffle of his fur, and raced out the door.

As her footsteps thundered down the stairs, Bobby looked at me. 'What about you?'

'Well, I've just written up my piece on the Bunny Bandit.' Bobby's eyebrow tilted, questioning me.

'It was stealing from its owners,' I clarified.

A slight smirk twisted on his lips. 'Is that a step up or step down from Claudine Rosso?' he grinned.

I bit the inside of my cheek, grateful that my fangs weren't out. Claudine Rosso was the red panda, and I'd told Bobby in no uncertain terms that it had been a low point in my journalistic career. Of course, that had been before the mango hooch seagulls.

'Pretty much on par,' I said.

'Welcome to small town living,' he laughed back at me. 'Now, whatcha got planned for this afternoon? A Houdini hamster to write up, maybe? Or a piece on a typewriting tortoise? Though I doubt he'd have particularly fast typing skills.' He guffawed at his own jokes. I offered him a withering glare in response.

'Not at the minute, actually. If it was okay with you, I was going to head down and visit Alex at the station. He messaged earlier asking if I could drop in and talk about The Guardians. He was going to ring around his sources at the weekend. I was hoping he'd have a little more info.'

The Guardians were the name of the vampire trafficking group responsible for my current state, and it was safe to say I wasn't one of their favourite people. I'd staked one of their members, killed another potential recruit, and then had the memories wiped of the final two recruits, so they wouldn't remember any of it. As much as I wished it wasn't the case, there was a very good chance they were going to come after me for that.

So my plan was to get to them first. If that was even possible.

'I'll walk out with you,' Bobby said. 'I'm meeting June for lunch. Could do with a bit of fresh air to clear my head and everything.'

'Sounds good.'

As I grabbed Pongo's leash, my boss turned to the remaining two left in the office.

'I guess you guys are holding down the fort here,' he said.

'Fine with me,' Theodora replied.

'Don't get up to anything too bad while we're gone,' he added, this time looking at Diego.

'Or if you do, at least make sure it's something worthwhile to put in the paper,' I interjected. 'I really need to write a decent article.'

Bobby rolled his single eye in my direction.

'You high-flyers... you just don't know how to take a rest, do you?'

'Nope.' I grinned back as I packed up Pongo's buttons into my bag so I could take them with us. 'Now come on. I've got some research to do.'

THREE

W hilst I hadn't got used to every aspect of my vampire life, or my move to the Ravens Hollow Oracle, one thing I had got used to on this side of the planet was the weather.

I'd grown up in England and spent most of my life in London, where drizzle was almost guaranteed on the weather forecast each day. Which, to be fair, was a good thing, because that was the only kind of weather Brits could cope with.

There was no aircon in the houses for when it got too hot. And as for the cold? We didn't get that crisp, white snow you could build snowmen from, like they did in other parts of Europe. No, we got slush. And we'd be lucky if it lasted a day. Of course, schools and airports still had to close, because we couldn't get the roads gritted or cleared, and I still had no idea why that was. Then again, maybe I was being a bit unfair to British weather. After all, it could be absolutely stunning. The only problem was that happened for about three weeks a year, though whether those three weeks would come in May or September or any of the weeks between was anyone's guess, though you could almost guarantee it wasn't the same three weeks that everyone had booked off for their summer holiday.

Here, though, I'd had blue skies, warm sun, and a breeze drifting in from the sea, tinged with a taste of salt air every day since my arrival. Of course, we were heading into hurricane season soon.

'How's life at the station?' I asked Bobby as we headed outside. His daughter Raquel was an officer there, and one of our key sources.

'Yeah, she doesn't talk to me about work unless she needs to,' Bobby said. 'What about the boss? Any idea when he'll be back? Alex has been holding down the fort for a while now.'

The boss was Chief Inspector Whip. The outrageously attractive cursed siren, who had been called off the island only a couple of days after I'd woken up from my mermaid attack.

'No idea,' I said, trying to sound as casual as possible.

'You not heard from him?' Bobby asked.

'I've heard from him now and then.'

I had promised myself that in moving to Ravens Hollow, I would steer clear of all men. My previous relationship back in London had all gone to dust when I was changed into a vampire. And as such, I'd put a pause on romance. That had been the plan, at least... until I arrived here and met the men at the police station, including Chief Inspector Whip.

It wasn't just a case of him being gorgeous, though he absolutely was. He also did sweet things, like finding a dog bed for Pongo, along with taking shifts at my bedside while I was out of it due to the mermaid venom. Then there was the minute detail about him placing a ward on me so that I was no longer affected by his siren powers. Yup, he was an incredibly rare male siren. Not only that, but one who had been cursed, so that he was now also immortal. His powers meant that he could influence people's thoughts, and it was fair to say I'd had some very unprofessional thoughts when I'd first met him. But then he'd got Nyrah to do the ward, so now when the thought of kissing him entered my mind, it was because I wanted to, not because he'd put the idea there.

Ravens Hollow was his home, and he'd told me before that he had no intention of moving anywhere else, but he'd been called off the island for an extended conference into organised crime in the magical community, only two days after finally asking me on a date. It was meant to be two weeks long, but there had been more to discuss than anticipated. Apparently, the head of the mermaid mafia escaping from prison had caused them to push a fair few more items onto the agenda. And as said mermaid had come to Ravens Hollow, there was no way Whip could sneak out early. So, as for when he was going to return and take me on that date he'd promised, I had no idea.

Since he'd been gone, he'd sent me a message every few days, just to check I was taking it easy, and to ask how Pongo's training was going. We hadn't reached the telephone conversation stage yet, but that was okay. I was happy to take things slow. And if we had spoken on the phone, I suspect I would have had to deal with his worry.

I'd planned on keeping my incident with The Guardians a secret. The last thing I wanted was for them to find out where I was and come after me. But secrets and small towns are like feral cats and bathtime. It doesn't matter how much you want them, the two just don't work together. So as much as I'd liked to believe that The Guardians still didn't know where I was, the likelihood was slim. And Whip had made it perfectly clear that he wanted nothing more than to keep me locked away from trouble, at least until he was back, but I'd gone for a different approach – trying to expose The Guardians before they could get to me. And thankfully, Alex had been on hand to help me.

Alex was the antithesis of Whip, and not just because of his blond surfer good looks and lilting Irish accent. He was easy going. Always ready to make me laugh. But at the same time, so hardworking. He had been looking into The Guardians for years, after a spate of sireless vampires had turned up in a town he was previously living in. Given my personal interest, along with the desire to get a well-deserved story out of everything The Guardians had put me through, the joint interest had seen us spending a lot of time together the past couple of weeks. And the more time I spent with him, the more I enjoyed his company. As much as I enjoyed Whip's...? That was a question I didn't want to think about too much.

'Well, I'm sure we'll hear from our chief inspector soon enough,' Bobby said, breaking the silence.

Yup, I lost way too much time thinking about those two men. 'Right,' I said, clearing my throat. 'I'm sure he'll be back when he can.'

'I'm sure you can keep yourself occupied until he's back. How is Alex, by the way? Raquel really likes working with him. And I hear he likes working with you, too.'

A smirk twisted Bobby's lips. I was at least ninety-nine percent sure my boss didn't have mind-reading abilities, but it was the one percent that made me nervous. Then again, maybe I just wasn't as good at hiding my confusion about the men in my life as I liked to think.

'Are you meeting June here for lunch, or going some-where else?' I said, fully aware how unsubtle my change of subject was. 'You don't want to be late.'

We had paused outside a familiar building. So familiar I rarely spent a day without a visit, and other than dog food, this was where the vast majority of my salary went. While Weirdoughs wasn't the only place to get food on the island – there were several restaurants and bars down by the beach, most of which I still hadn't visited – this was the one we tended to frequent the most, and not only because it was the closest to the paper, but because of the extra shots they would add to the coffees and food. Extra shots I and the other vampires of the island were incredibly grateful for.

'I 'spect she's already inside,' Bobby answered. 'You comin' in and grabbing a coffee or heading straight off?'

Pongo tugged at my lead, pulling me towards the door. He, too, was a fan of the snacks they served here, and all the staff now knew him by name. As did a surprising number of island residents.

'It'd be rude not to, since I'm here,' I said, stepping forward and opening the door so Bobby could step inside.

Sure, I could've drunk blood from a blood bag. Maybe even found a witch to spell it to taste differently, like my best friend Donna had done in England. But I much preferred it with a shot of caffeine, and occasionally caramel syrup, too.

Given the proximity to midday, it was unsurprising that a hefty queue had formed in front of the takeaway section of the bakery. So while Bobby went to find June, I joined the back of the snaking line, only to find myself directly behind a familiar face.

'Ines,' I said. 'How's it going?'

'Hey, Elodie.' The werewolf beta was dressed in her typical outfit of leather boots, jeans, and an oversized T-shirt, though it was the coloured glow of her eyes that was her most identifiable feature. Amber. Just like the pack she belonged to. Ines was one of these women who exuded comfort in her own skin. Her very presence felt connected with nature. Assuming you ignored the slight hint of formaldehyde to her scent. Not that it was her fault; her aunt was a taxidermy fan, who insisted that Ines keep some of her works on display in the house she shared with her sister. 'How's it going?'

'Pretty slow,' I replied. 'What about you?'

She rolled those amber eyes of hers as she let out a sigh. 'Frustrating,' she said. 'It was a full moon last week. The woods we've been allowed to hunt have been so stripped some of my pack almost ended up in the Scorched Circle. Including Sophia.'

Sophia was Ines's younger sister and while my first question should probably have been to check she was alright, it was another one that came out of my mouth first.

'The Scorched Circle?' I said. 'What's that?'

Ines's eyes narrowed, though she ordered her drink before responding.

'You don't know the Scorched Circle?'

'Still pretty new here, remember?'

'Sorry. Right, of course,' she shook her head. 'Let's just say it's not the type of place you want to end up.'

That didn't help. I was living on an island inhabited by paranormals. There wasn't a single area of the woodland I'd have wanted to end up on a full moon now I knew werewolves were a real thing. I had no idea what kind of creatures would have to live in this Scorched Circle to freak out werewolves.

'A lot of the packs are seriously angry now. And not just mine,' she continued. 'The wood sprites are making it really difficult for us to hunt. Throwing spells out to distract our sense of smell, that type of thing. And I can hardly blame them. It's their home, and there's space in other parts of the island we can use. And they don't have the luxury of up and moving.'

'I put everything you'd proposed to the council in an article last week,' I said. 'Hoping it would push them into making a decision.'

Ines nodded as she offered me a weak smile. 'I saw, thank you. Hopefully, next meeting they'll have an answer. But I suspect they'll just delay it.'

'Then I'll just write two articles in the next paper. One on the hunting regulations and one on the sluggishness of the council. I promise, I'll do everything I can. Maybe we could even get some of the wood sprites to do us a quote. If they can do, that is?' I wasn't even sure if they could speak.

Ines smile widened. 'Thank you, Elodie. I really appreciate it.'

'Green tea and a meat feast sandwich?' The barista said

'That's me.' Ines reached out and took the drink and paper bag. 'See you soon? Though maybe not with a wood sprite. You'd have to find someone braver than me to talk to them. Those teeth. Those wings.' She shuddered. 'Scary. See you, Pongo.'

I chuckled to myself. A fully grown werewolf and beta of a pack, nervous of a tiny sprite? I guess it was like humans being scared of a spider.

Three minutes later, I was walking out of Weirdoughs with my drink, Pongo chewing on a treat from the jar they kept on the counter. The plan was still to head towards the police station and talk to Alex about The Guardians, but I pulled out my phone and scrolled down the list of contacts until I reached the Mayor's office.

I had promised I would do everything I could, and that meant holding the council responsible for dragging their heels with regulations that were affecting people's lives. And there was no time like the present to do that.

FOUR

As Pongo continued to enjoy his chew, I took a seat on a nearby bench

While my phone was answered by the mayor's office quick enough, getting through to the woman herself was decidedly more difficult.

'I'm afraid the mayor's unable to take calls right now,' the person on the end of the line said.

'Unable, or unwilling?' I said. They cleared their throat, no doubt ready to offer me a quick retort, but I got in there before they could. 'You see, I tried to get hold of her yesterday and the day before. It's Elodie Evergreen, remember? From the Oracle. And I'll be honest, the fact that the mayor doesn't have time to even hold a single conversation with the only paper on the island – the one way her constituents have to see information disseminated – is pretty concerning. Is it me she's avoiding, or is it facing her constituents?'

'I can assure you the mayor is not avoiding anyone.'

'Well then, you'll put her on the phone, won't you? Because I'm standing outside the office right now, and it would be much better for everyone if I didn't have to come up there and make a scene, because that would definitely make front page news, don't you think?'

It was a barefaced lie. I was on the other side of town, but the person on the end of the line didn't know that. A click flittered down the line, as if she was clicking her jaw.

'I'll just see if she's free.' When the voice spoke this time, it was with a definite edge.

'That would be great, thank you,' I said.

A moment later, and my phone call was being transferred to a mayor who all of a sudden had just five minutes free to talk.

'Ms Evergreen.' Her voice grated with annoyance. I'd hardly had any dealings with the mayor, but from what little I knew, I wasn't her biggest fan. Not only had she and the council allowed Wren Belkin, the egg smuggler slash sculptor, to exhibit on the island, they'd also kicked several other artists out of their deserved spots to do so.

'Mayor Hillard, hello. So glad you managed to find a minute to squeeze in talking to me.' She grunted in response, and a feeling of satisfaction rippled through me. 'I was just wondering if you'd got an update on the new regulations of hunting grounds for the packs? Obviously, it's been three weeks since the meeting. I was hoping I could put an update in the paper this week. Unless you want another no comment? I'm sure I can get plenty of quotes from people who've been affected to fill up the article if you'd rather. I hear some wood sprites are very keen to go on record.'

The Mayor clicked her tongue. Was I deliberately getting on her nerves by telling a couple of white lies? Yes. Was it a sensible idea? If it kicked her and the council into motion, then absolutely.

'We're getting there, Ms Evergreen. But, as people who've been in the paranormal community longer know, these things take time.'

'You're right. I'm new here,' I said. 'Unlike the residents who have brought these complaints to you. I'm sure you know they're born and bred Ravens Hollow.' She let out a slight huff, but just like with her assistant, I didn't give her a chance to respond before I continued. 'Any idea how much time? A date? You've got a lot of people who are keen to get this through.'

'I'm aware, yes. But by "people," you mean werewolves.'

I locked my jaw together. 'Even as someone who is *new* to Ravens Hollow, I'm aware of the wider impact on the community, Mayor. Shifters. Sprites. All creatures that live off the land. The werewolves might be the most vocal about it, but I can assure you they are not the only people affected by this refusal to allow hunting in Folorning Forest.'

A sharp sniff preceded the mayor's next words. 'Well, in my position I have to think of *all* the inhabitants of the island. Not only the creatures who inhabit our woodland.'

A smile curled my lips. 'By *all* the inhabitants, I

assume you're talking about the wealthiest residents of the island, who live in Pepper's Bay. The same Pepper's Bay where the houses risk decreasing in value if wolves and shifters hunt on that land behind it. You, yourself are one of those residents, are you not? Are those the inhabitants that you're thinking of?'

'That is absolute nonsense,' she hissed, only for my smile to widen. Yup, there was something incredibly satisfying at riling up someone like Mayor Hillard.

For the next two minutes, I listened to her throw jargon at me, in what I'm sure she believed was a convincing argument. But the thing was, I'd been at the town meeting, listening to Ines and Sophia Ortega talk about this at length, with *actual* understanding. I hadn't known when I first met the sisters, but they both had degrees in mythological ecology, and Ines was currently working on her thesis on the same topic. She was a damn intelligent woman, and when it came to ecosystems – especially magical ones – I was tempted to believe her over Mayor Hillard, whose own master's degree was in Public Policy and Optics. Perfect for her current role and being able to spin enough of a line to win her some votes, but not for dishing out advice on the island's ecosystem.

'So there's no progress to print in this week's paper? That's what you're telling me, Mayor? Anything you'd like to quote? I don't know... a time estimate?'

She let out a long sigh before offering me some trite line about 'balance,' 'duty,' and 'responsibility.'

'I would thank you,' I said when she finally finished. 'But it's not like you've actually done anything to help any of your constituents with this issue, is it?' With that, I ended the call.

It was my turn to let out a sigh, at which Pongo lifted up his paw and rested it on my knee before letting out two barks. We had worked a lot on our commands, but ninety percent of the time, he insisted on barking twice after any action, like those people who always finished a sentence with the word 'right.'

'I'm fine,' I said. 'Come on, time to go to the station. And you know what that means, don't you?'

Pongo's tail began to wag so hard it slapped against the side of my leg.

'Alright, calm down. We'll go see your buddy, assuming she's there, that is.' I let out a little chuckle to myself, knowing full well that Pongo's number one play-mate would be at the station. It wasn't like she could go anywhere else. She was a ghost.

I didn't know why I found Pongo's friendship with Josephina so amusing. I was currently great friends with a fae, a werewolf, and whatever the heck the other paras at the office were. But somehow that made more sense to me than Pongo and Josephina.

The moment the station came into view, Pongo upped his pace. We'd spent a fair amount of time at the station over the last couple of weeks. Alex had invited me over to look at what he'd got on the Guardian traffickers, and while I wanted to give Pongo plenty of attention and play with him the entire time, that just wasn't possible. Not when I was trying to go through dates and facts. And so, Josephina had taken over the role of chief Pongo entertainer when we were at the station.

There were a lot of things she couldn't do, obviously. She couldn't play fetch with him. She couldn't take snacks out of the large jar that Alex kept on his desk for when we came over to visit. But she could do things that

I, or any other being with a corporeal status, could not manage. Like running through the desks, or disappearing into one wall, only to reappear behind Pongo a second later.

And he loved it.

However, trying to get work done when you had no idea when a ghost or a dog would careen towards you was easier said than done. Fortunately, as Pongo was still only a pup, half an hour of chaos was normally enough to tire him out. Alex and I used the time to chat about general day-to-day goings on and learn a little bit about one another's lives before Ravens Hollow – not that there was much to know about mine – before Pongo collapsed by my feet and fell asleep, normally for a solid hour, during which we would get on with our research in earnest.

Thankfully, Raquel didn't seem to mind the disruption, though I had wondered more than once whether we would continue to work in such a manner once Whip was back and in charge of the station. Was he the type of man who would cope with a dog and ghost playing chase through his office? He was the one who had given Josephina an actual role at the station, after she had spent years haunting the people who worked there, and he had never given the impression of not liking dogs. But did that mean he wanted one running through his workspace? It was hard to know anything.

Then again, once he was back, Alex would have more time off and we would be able to meet up outside of the station. In a purely professional manner.

Yes, Alex was gorgeous. And sweet and funny. But we were working together, and I didn't want to do anything that screwed up my chances of finding the ringleaders to The Guardians. Besides, from the way his phone constantly buzzed, he was more than a bit of a player, and there was no chance I wanted to risk my heart with someone like that. And there was Whip to think of. Whip, who had asked me to hold on until he was back in Ravens Hollow, and we could recommence whatever it was we had almost started, as if he was worried I'd start seeing someone else in his absence.

When I reached the station. I could barely hold Pongo back as I opened the door, ready for him and Josephina to start their ridiculous games before I'd even got his leash off.

But as I stepped inside, the ghost didn't immediately jump out in front to begin her games, the way she normally did. Instead she was occupied.

As well as listening to the answering machines – she couldn't actually pick up the telephone, so had to recall the messages after they had been left – Josephina's other role in the station was as a receptionist of sorts, finding out why people had come, so that she could relay the information to the team and sort the situation out accordingly. Although at that moment, it seemed that the woman in front of her had come in with the sole intention of shouting loudly.

'It's disgusting and it's diabolical, and something needs to be done about it!' she shouted. 'Immediately!'

While the woman had her back to me, there was

something familiar about her dark auburn hair, although it was her jumper of the exact same shade that made me realise what I was looking at: a jumper made from her own fur.

'Did you hear me?' she continued. 'This needs sorting. Now, are you going to whizz through that wall and find someone who can actually help me, or do I have to go there myself?'

'Mrs Rosso?' I said.

The woman swivelled around, and sure enough, I found myself face to face with the red-panda-shifter who I had written an entire article on the week before, albeit in her human form. Unlike our last meeting when she had beamed for photos holding up her creations – which were all shades of auburn, with occasional accents of white and black – there was no hint of a smile on her face. Her teeth were gritted in a near snarl that only tightened when she looked at me.

'You!' she said, pointing a finger at me. 'Of course you'd be here. This is all your fault. You hear me? You and that paper of yours are not going to get away with this!'

A s a journalist, I've been told things were my fault more than once.

Earlier in my career, it had been my fault that marriages broke down when I uncovered stories about a cheating politician or celebrity. Always mine, not the spouse who was sleeping around. When I'd moved into less sleazy investigations, it had been my fault when clubs or facilities had shut down after I reported on people on the boards embezzling funds or substandard buildings or safety policies. I'd also been blamed for people losing their jobs in those same situations. Yes, this definitely wasn't the first time I'd been blamed unfairly.

But I struggled to see what I could have done to upset Mrs Rosso. Previously, she'd been more than happy for us to write all about her hobby, even offering to do a follow-up piece on how to spin fur into yarn.

'Look at this.' She pointed to three large bags around

her feet, one of which Pongo was already sticking his nose into. By the looks – and smell – of it, it appeared to be fur.

'I'm sorry Mrs Rosso?' I say in confusion. 'What is it? What's happened exactly?'

'What's wrong? What's happened?' She shook her head and scoffed. 'This is elk fur! Do you have any idea how much an elk moults? Bags and bags of it, all over my porch. And it stinks!'

Yup, it really did.

Pongo had got his name not just because I was a fan of the classic 101 Dalmatians, but because when I'd first found him he'd smelt so bad that Bobby had refused to let him into his truck and I'd had to carry him home. I'd washed the clothes I'd worn holding him on a hot wash twice afterwards, but whether it was my imagination or not, his smell seemed embedded into the fibres. I'd ended up donating the top to a charity.

'Apparently, your little article made everybody think that I would just love all their moultings,' Mrs Rosso raged. 'Well, I do not love all their moultings. I do not want all their moultings. What I want is to make a formal complaint against you and that paper of yours, that allowed this to happen.' She spun back around to face Josephina. 'Now, can you find someone who can do that for me? Or do I have to make a complaint about you too?'

Josephina's eyebrows lifted a good two inches higher, as did her entire body, as she rose several inches into the air to look down her nose at Mrs Rosso. And I couldn't say I blamed her.

'You want to make a complaint about me?' she said, her voice a low tremble. 'Me? Who has failed to be claimed by death herself. Who has the ability to speak to souls in that realm and the next, and could ensure that every waking and sleeping moment of your life is haunted by such apparitions? You wish to complain about the spectre of the station? The poltergeist of the precinct? You want to complain about me? I'd like to see you try.'

I had to give it to her. Pongo's best friend could be mighty terrifying.

To give Mrs Rosso her due, she didn't crumble into a quivering wreck the way I suspect I would have done had Josephina's ghostly wrath been directed at me. But before she had a chance to respond, Josephina let out a high shriek, disappearing into the wall with a wail.

Next to me, Pongo let out a loud bark before rushing up to the door and striking it with his paws, clearly thinking the games had begun. Yet rather than Josephina reappearing, it was Raquel who came out into reception.

'Is everything okay?' she said. Her gaze shifted first to Pongo, then me, and finally to Mrs Rosso.

'No!' Mrs Rosso glowered. 'Everything is not okay. First off, you are running a mighty unprofessional setup, and secondly, thanks to this woman, I'm getting all kind of furs dumped on my porch. I want it stopped, and the paper held responsible for the distress it has caused me.'

Raquel shot me a quick glance, and all I could do was

offer her a half-hearted shrug. Did I expect people to dump their fur on Mrs Rosso's door because I wrote an article about her jumpers? No. But was it really as bad as she made it sound?

'Exactly how many bags have been dumped?' I said.

'Hundreds!' she said with exasperation. 'Well, it looks like hundreds. I didn't know exactly. I didn't count them all, but at least forty.'

Okay, that did sound like quite a lot.

Raquel offered me a slight smile that was accompanied by a roll of her eyes, as if to imply this was the type of crap she had to deal with day in and day out.

'Right you are, Mrs Rosso,' she said. 'Why don't you come through and talk to me? I'll take some notes.' As she opened the door for Mrs Rosso to step through, Raquel threw a glance over her shoulder at me.

'Alex is in there,' she said. 'Assuming it's him you're looking for.'

'Thank you.' I turned to follow her into the office, only for Josephina to reappear.

'The nerve of that woman,' she muttered. 'Thinking she could make a complaint about me.' She crouched down and held her arms out for Pongo, who barked with delight as he ran straight through her.

'Are you all right if I leave him here with you, Josephina?'

'Oh, no problem at all,' the old ghost said with a wave of her hand. 'We'll be absolutely fine, won't we, Pongo? Now, let's see if you can catch me this time.'

CHAPTER
SEVEN

Despite the number of times I had been in the police station, there were countless areas of the building where I had no idea what went on. I knew that Whip had an apartment upstairs that could be accessed via a door behind reception, and that there were cells and interview rooms off the main office area. But it was in the central open plan space with its low-walled cubicles where I spent most of my time, and that was where I found Alex, typing away at his computer.

'Hey, are you busy? I can come back later if you are?' I asked.

Alex, I now knew, was a lion shifter, which made sense, given the thick blond mane of hair that was currently tied back behind his head. He was a beast of a man, but when he looked up at me and grinned, it was also clear that he was a complete softy.

'Hey, Evergreen. You know I always have time for

you. Although I just saw Raquel bringing Mrs Rosso back. I'm sure she's got it handled, but I'll need to keep an ear out, in case it kicks off.'

'With Mrs Rosso?' The woman barely came up to my shoulders. And sure, she was a dab hand with knitting needles, but Raquel was half-siren, half(suspected)-cyclops. I really couldn't imagine there was much she couldn't handle.

'Oh, Claudine just loves the drama. Anyway...' Alex reached out and pulled a chair from the next desk over to his. 'I'm glad you're here. I wanted to show you this.'

There was no general chitchat today then. Straight to work. I took a seat.

'Okay, so I know it's messy, but I think the best thing we can do is assume that all vampires who have undeclared sires in the last hundred and fifty-years have been changed by The Guardians. Right?'

I had learned only a few weeks ago that siring a vampire – while simple physically, was a bureaucratic nightmare. The hefty administrative aspect had been put into place a hundred and fifty years ago, hence Alex's choice in date.

'Obviously, that method is flawed, because there are always one or two outliers, but around fifteen years ago, the number suddenly shot up, from a couple a year to a couple a month and then a week. If we look globally, it's probably a couple a day now.'

The statistic caused me to let out a long exhale. Over seven hundred new vampires a year?

'Eight sireless have been recorded in the system from

across the world this week,' he said. 'But if they're all coming from The Guardians, then they're being smart about it. These vamps have appeared all the way from New England to New Zealand. No two in the same country.'

I took a moment to think. 'That doesn't make sense, though,' I said. 'When I was investigating missing people in London, it was several people going missing each month. And we know The Guardians were behind that.'

'Yeah, I know.' He pressed his lips together in a way that told me he'd already thought of that. "All brawn and no brains" were the first words that had come into my head when I'd first met Alex, although they hadn't actually been my thoughts. They'd been put there accidentally by Whip, when he'd jealously assumed we'd start flirting. He'd admitted it to me later on, when he'd also told me that Alex was one of the smartest people he knew. And the more time I spent with Alex, the easier I found it to believe that. The man had serious depths. He just did a good job of keeping them hidden.

'I think it's all deliberate,' Alex continued. 'They hold them somewhere. Maybe for months. Maybe for years. Then they drop them off nowhere near where they were taken from, making it nearly impossible to tell where they've come from.'

'Unless we find them and they tell us?' I suggested.

He shrugged. 'I suspect they're under strict instructions not to tell anyone, at the risk of their lives. When someone's risked that much to become a vamp, I struggle to believe they'd give it up easily. They might have even had their memory erased so they can't.'

He was right. I knew it. But if we could find one who would? Just one, of all these vamps being changed, then maybe they could tell us where they were held before being taken to a para community. Or who they were there with. I was sure Nyrah, the strongest of the local witches, would be able to break through any spells that had been placed on them. But maybe I was just being hopeful.

'Do we have any in Ravens Hollow?' I asked. 'Any sireless?'

He shook his head. 'No, I already checked. You can see for yourself.'

He moved his mouse and clicked through a couple of windows until a new screen appeared in front of us, though the font was so small, I needed to lean across him so I could get a better view of the screen. My arm brushed against his, and it was hard not to notice the rise in his heartbeat. Or the way his breath quickened.

At first, I'd assumed the way Alex flirted with me was the way he flirted with everyone, but the more time we spent together, the more I realised that wasn't the case. The hastening of his pulse. The dilation of his pupils. Maybe human me would have been oblivious to the signs, but vampire me was well aware that there was some definite attraction, and sometimes I couldn't help but question whether spending time with him was a good idea. But he knew we were just friends. Whip and I had a connection. Even if I hadn't seen him for weeks.

It was only when Alex cleared his throat that I realised I hadn't said anything. As a slight heat filled my cheeks, I refocused my attention back on the computer. I hadn't realised how many vamps there were living in Ravens Hollow and was about to say as much, but as I opened my mouth, I was cut off by a familiar voice.

'I'm not interrupting anything, am I?'

I turned around, sure my impeccable hearing had to be playing games with me, but as my eyes landed on the perfect green of his irises, my jaw fell open.

'Whip,' I said, already on my feet. 'You're back.'

I met Whip the night I had first arrived in Ravens Hollow when he'd broken up a small group of protestors, including Ines and Sophia. The Chief Inspector left me a little tongue-tied, although that wasn't entirely my fault. His power, as a cursed male siren, is to bend other people's thoughts to his will, and it was a power he thought he had under control until he'd met me. But it's safe to say we both had pretty strong reactions to seeing each other.

Now, though, when I got tongue-tied from seeing him, I knew it was all my own fault.

'You didn't say you were coming back,' I said, as I moved towards him.

'No. Well, it was pretty last minute.'

His eyes glinted. I was standing about a third of the way across the room from him, aching with the urge to reach up on tiptoes and kiss him – or at least hug him – but I wasn't quite sure where we were. A lot could change in four weeks. Maybe he'd met somebody off island. Another police officer.

I could hear Alex's heart pounding a slight grinding noise, as if he was annoyed Whip had turned up when he did. It was all rather messy, but one thing was for certain. Whip looked good.

'I saw Pongo playing with Josephina out in reception,' Whip said, his eyes still locked on mine. 'Looks like they get on well.'

'They do,' I said. 'He's spent a lot of time here. You know, while Alex and I are together.'

Something flickered across Whip's expression and caused my non-existent pulse to skitter. Jealousy perhaps?

Was it wrong of me that I was happy he would still feel jealous about me?

'We've been looking into The Guardians,' I said, not sure why there was such a large lump lodged in my throat. 'That's all. That's the only reason I'm here, spending time with him.'

'Wow, Evergreen,' Alex said, letting out a low whistle as he stood up. 'You sure know how to make a guy feel special.'

I winced. If I'd still had normal, pumping blood, I was pretty sure it would've coloured my cheeks in a deep blush. Instead, I just offered him an apologetic glance. 'Sorry, Alex, I didn't mean—'

'I'm winding you up, Evergreen,' he said, slipping past me to offer Whip a hug. 'Good to have you back, boss. I've left you all the paperwork. I know it's your favourite.'

Whip rolled his eyes as he grinned.

'You're the person in the office who actually likes paperwork and spreadsheets.'

It was Alex's turn to wince. 'I like things organised. Is that a crime?' He chuckled before shifting his attention back to me. 'I think I'm gonna see if Raquel needs any help. This office feels awfully crowded right now.'

'Crowded? But there's only the three of u—' I stopped myself with a shake of the head as I realised what he was doing. 'Yeah. Right. Thanks.'

A moment later, he was gone, and Whip and I were alone.

Though if Alex thought it would get less awkward, he was very wrong. Instead, Whip and I continued to stare at each other in complete silence, the lump in my throat refusing to budge. Was he expecting me to speak first? I couldn't tell. It felt that way.

'I hope you've been okay..'

'I hope everything went okay.'

We spoke simultaneously, then stopped at the exact same time too.

'Go on—'

'Sorry, I shouldn't have—'

'No, you go,' I said.

'It's fine. It's just...' He paused, clearing his throat before continuing. 'I was just going to say I was sorry I couldn't get back sooner. Things off island were a little...' He hesitated, searching for the right word. 'Complicated. My sister turned up at the conference on the last day.'

'Your sister? She's in the force too? I didn't know. '

I didn't know much about Whip's life before Ravens Hollow. In fact, I knew close to nothing, but I did know that the woman he referred to as his sister, was in fact a vampire, who'd been turned by the same person who cursed him.

Being a male siren was rare – *one in every two hundred years* – type rare. That was why he was cursed to be an immortal weapon. One that could make someone do his master's bidding with just a twist of the mind. His sister was turned by the same evil villain. I assumed the pair of them were no longer in contact with said being, but it wasn't like we were at that point in our relationship where I could ask him about that. I mean, I couldn't even ask him if we were in a relationship.

'So, you and Alex—'

'We've been trying to track down The Guardians. That's all,' I said, cutting him off before he could say more, but this time, a smile flashed across his face, revealing a singular dimple on his left side. God, that dimple was so damn cute.

'I was just about to ask if you've made any progress. That's all.'

My stomach flipped, then settled into an impressively tight knot. In all of my human years, I couldn't remember a single time when a man had got me as flustered as I became when I was talking to Whip, and that was with the ward. But it was probably because we hadn't seen each other for so long. Perhaps I'd manage to get a grip on it after we'd spent some proper time together. Not that I was sure if I wanted to get a grip on it. There was something about the giddiness that was damn near intoxicating.

'We were just looking at sireless vampires, but it's hard to find the links to The Guardians. It's just lots of numbers, but no patterns yet.'

'Well, if anyone can work it out, it's you two. I'm sure of it.'

His eyes locked on mine and the fluttering that filled my abdomen reached a whole new level. After my previous dating disasters, I still found it hard to believe that a guy like Whip was genuinely interested in me. A workaholic, newly-turned vampire who really had very little idea what she was doing with her life. But he did. He was. At least, the way he was looking at me said he was.

'I'm sorry that we didn't have that date before I left,' he said, that dimple still in place. 'I wondered if maybe you'd be free tonight?'

'Tonight?' Wow. That wasn't wasting any time.

'Well, I felt like we've waited long enough.' He took a step towards me. 'Assuming you still want to, that is, you don't—'

'Yes. Yes,' I said. Clearly, I wasn't one of those women who acted cool. Then again, why would I want to be? I was me. It had taken a lot of work, particularly after my mother, Maria, left us, but now, I was at a point where I liked the person I was. And I wasn't going to change myself, no matter how cute that dimple was.

'Tonight sounds good,' I said, trying to sound a little

more casual. Though from the grin that flashed in Whip's eyes, he didn't buy it for a second.

'Why don't I pick you up for dinner at seven?' he said. 'How does that sound?'

This wasn't a daydream. This was genuinely real. The most attractive man I'd ever seen in my life was really planning on taking me on a date tonight. I opened my mouth, willing a coherent answer to come out. But before I could say a word, there was a rush of air, so fast it sent papers flying from the desk.

'Josephina!' Whip spun around, recognising the sudden wind for what it was a moment before I did. 'Can you not knock?' Whip said.

She offered him a withering look.

'Quite frankly, I find that remark hurtful,' she pouted. 'I would have thought someone in your position would have more sensitivity.'

Whip let out a restrained sigh. 'You're right, Josephina. I'm sorry. Is there something you wanted?'

'Obviously,' she replied. 'There's a message on the phone and it sounds important. I think you need to go listen.'

Whip looked at me, but I nodded. 'Go. It's fine.'

As he opened the door to reception, Pongo bounded through, offering me a quick wag of his tail before racing after Josephina. Obviously, he thought the change in the room was part of the game.

Suspecting that it was time for us to get out of there – with every member of the station now occupied with police work – I grabbed Pongo's leash to walk him home, when Whip reappeared.

'Is everything okay?' I said. From the pinched lines of his cheeks and the way his lips were pressed together, it certainly didn't look great.

'Did you drive?' he said. 'Did you drive over here?'

I shook my head. 'No, I walked Pongo over from the paper.'

'Right, then in that case, you need to come in the car with me. Josephina,' he said, turning to the apparition. 'Get Alex too. Tell him to follow us.'

'Righty-ho boss,' she said, whizzing through the wall in the direction of the questioning rooms.

While Josephina disappeared, Whip opened the door to his office, then unlocked a large cabinet from which he gathered several items that he dropped into a large satchel. I had seen Whip in work mode before, when he had been trying to track down a murderer.

The scent of a story was tingling every nerve in my body. The handsome chief inspector and I were officially going on a date, and there might be a headline worth investigating on the horizon. Could the day get any better? Still, I tried to keep my excitement under wraps as I next spoke.

'Whip, what is it? What's happened?'

As Whip fixed his eyes on mine, fear flashed in those perfect green irises.

'It's Diego,' he said, zipping up the bag. 'Something's happened to Diego.'

NINE

'What did they say, exactly?' I jumped into the car next to Whip. Clearly, the fact that Pongo didn't make a fuss in being relegated to the back seat was a sign that he understood the urgency of the situation. Or at the very least, could feel the panic rising off his owner. 'You're sure it's Diego, not someone else.'

'Another of the Lapiz wolves rang it in,' Whip said. The Lapiz wolves were Diego's pack, dispelling any hope I had that my colleague had been falsely identified. 'They just said he was causing chaos. Walking straight down the middle of the road, like he couldn't even see the traffic.'

While Ravens Hollow was the only town on the island, there were several small hamlets where the wolf packs lived. There was also the exclusive development of homes over by Pepper's Bay. But there was only one main road, aptly named Bridge Road, that lead directly to the bridge to the mainland and bisected the entire island. Whether you were going in or out, you would always use Bridge Road at some point. Every other road and track branched off it. If Diego was walking down that, then chaos would be the last thing we need to worry about. He would be lucky if he didn't get himself hit.

As we drove towards the north of the island, the traffic grew denser and slower until it eventually reached a complete standstill. People were beeping their horns, or getting out of their cars and waving angrily. Whip honked his horn, then put on his siren, causing several cars to shift to the side. The space they created allowed us to crawl forward, but I could have walked faster. And I wasn't talking about vamp speeding. I was talking very human Elodie, wearing high heels in the rain with shopping bags weighing her down as she tried not to stab someone with an umbrella.

'Wouldn't we be better getting out?' I said as I turned to Whip. 'I can run ahead. You know how fast I can go.'

'No Elodie,' He shook his head. 'It'll only take us a minute, I promise. I don't know what's up there.'

'I thought you said it was Diego. Diego's what's ahead of us, and if he's in trouble, then us sitting in traffic isn't going to help.'

I was trying to keep my voice measured, but it was hard. Diego wasn't just a colleague. He was a friend. A friend who ate all the banana cake Chloe made before the rest of us had a chance to get to it, and who'd be the first to cause a distraction and start gossiping in the office whenever he wasn't in the mood to work. And I couldn't just wait for traffic to clear if he needed me.

Whip pursed his lips.

'Sorry,' I said. 'I can't wait.' Without waiting for Whip to offer all the reasons as to why it was a bad idea, I jumped out of the car.

'Please, just be careful.'

I would have yelled back, only I was already too far away for him to hear.

As much as I wanted to go top speed, for that I needed a clear path, and with all the cars, that wasn't something I had. Still, it was faster than I would've been if I'd stayed stuck in the traffic.

The scent of pine needles filled my nose as we reached the outskirts of the Wraith Woods. As far as I was aware two wolf packs made this place their home and I was pretty sure Diego's wolves were amongst them. A moment later, the figure came into view, walking up in front of me.

'Diego...'

Even from the back, I knew who I was looking at. The werewolf was striding away down the middle of the road, close to the cars that were honking their horns, trying to get past.

'Diego!' I yelled again.

He didn't so much as flicker as he continued. I kicked up my speed and got in front of him, blocking his path.

'Diego!'

My voice cracked in my throat. Yes, I was looking at Diego, but there was something not right about him. His eyes were glazed, looking straight past me, as if I wasn't even there.

'People need to know,' he muttered quietly to himself. Repeating the same words over and over again at a volume that was barely audible, at least to normal hearing. That wasn't the only strange thing. There was an aroma rising from him, a syrupy sweetness. 'People need to know,' he repeated, his voice slipping into a slow growl. 'People need to know about us.'

'Diego, it's me. It's Elodie.' I reached my hand towards him, but he was continuing to walk forward. He would walk straight through me if I didn't move. Or would he? Maybe what he needed was something to shake him out of this. Like striding head on into a vampire. It was worth a try. I locked myself in position, ready for the impact. Diego closed in on me. He was short man, yes, but stocky too. Built like a boulder. And from the pace he was walking at would have a fair bit of momentum. Momentarily second guessing myself, I braced myself for the impact, when a jolt from the side threw me out of his path.

'Pongo?' I said. I knew my pup had grown, and sure I was caught by surprise, but it was a testament to how much that he was able to barrel me out of Diego's path. 'What are you doing? How did you get out of the car?'

'Elodie,' Whip was standing to the left of me. I turned to see him standing there, his face pinched. 'You need to step away from Diego. You need to get right out of the way.'

'I don't understand what's going on. It's like he can't hear me—'

'Elodie, you need to step away from him,' he repeated. 'Diego's been hexed.'

CHAPTER
TEN

I thought I'd got to grips with my vampire hearing issues, and even when I had experienced problems, it had been about deciphering where sounds came from. Not from mishearing. Yet I was sure I had to have misheard him. And yet when Whip spoke again, he said the exact same things.

'Diego's been hexed,' he repeated. 'Look at his hands.' I did as instructed, amazed that I hadn't noticed it before. Diego's normally pink flesh had taken on a green-brown tone and hard calloused texture. If anything, it looked more like tree bark than skin. 'You need to step away from him until we know how and why.'

Whip dropped his bag to the ground and pulled out a pair of cuffs. The dark grey metal was marked with black symbols and something told me they weren't your standard issue restraint.

'You're going to arrest him?' I said, a wave of anger

rippling through me. 'Whatever's going on, it's not his fault!'

'These are handcuffs are inscribed with runes,' Whip said as he unclipped them, ready for use. 'They block the wearer from being able to use any magic and shield them from being susceptible to magic, too. Meaning that, hopefully, they'll stop the hex from working.'

'Hopefully?' I repeated.

Whip didn't say any more to me. Instead, he took the cuffs and fixed his attention on Diego, clearly deliberating what his next move should be. Whip liked to think through his options, rather than acting on impulse, and while I admired that careful, considered approach, part of me wanted to grab the cuffs off him, and clip them onto Diego as quickly as possible, so this whole thing was over. But obviously, it wasn't that simple.

We were still on Bridge Road, but nearing the top end, surrounded by woods on either side. I could hear the beeping of car horns back from where we came, though none were approaching. I guessed Alex and Raquel were holding them back, and I was grateful. Whatever was going on with Diego, he deserved a little privacy.

'Hey, Diego,' Whip said now walking towards my werewolf colleague. 'I need you to stop. If you can hear me, then you have to stop, you understand? You have to stop. Now.'

I reckoned Whip was trying to use his siren's power to control Diego. I'd only seen snippets of it working before, when he'd broken up the protest, but he'd merely implied that he wanted the group to stop what they were doing, and they'd been powerless to refuse. This was a far more direct approach, and yet it didn't seem to be having any effect on Diego at all. His pace hadn't slowed by even a fraction and he was still muttering away to himself. Finally, Whip stopped talking, jumped into Diego's path, and clipped the runed cuffs around the werewolf's wrists.

A gasp broke from Diego's throat. For a split second, his eyes cleared, before they rolled back in his head. His jaw hung slack and his back arched as if his chest was being pulled up by an invisible thread. Whip stepped back, giving Diego a bit of space. Only that was the exact moment that the werewolf's knees buckled. Leaving Pongo where he was, I dived forward, catching Diego in my arms before he could hit the ground.

'Thanks. Good catch,' Whip said. 'You got him okay?'

I nodded. It still felt strange to me that I had no difficulty whatsoever catching a fully grown man, but that was an advantage to vampire strength. But however impressed I was with my reflexes and powers, it didn't stop the fear that was currently pumping through me.

'Was that supposed to happen?' I said, standing up and readjusting Diego's weight.

Whip bit down on his bottom lip, all traces of dimples gone. 'I've never seen them have that effect before,' he admitted. 'Whatever hexed him, I think it's powerful. I need to ring Vincent.'

The name was familiar. 'Vincent? Isn't that Nyrah's brother?'

Whip nodded. 'That's right. He works in magical medicine. He'll be able to get to the root of this. Hopefully, work out what kind of hex it is. And how we take it off him.'

I was still holding Diego upright, and it wasn't as if he was physically heavy, but the mental weight of seeing my friend in such a state was hard to bear.

'I was speaking to him just an hour ago,' I said. 'God. I need to ring Bobby. They need to know what's going on. They need—'

I stopped, my thoughts severed by a rustling sound to my right. An animal, perhaps? I sniffed the air, but from the rabbits and chipmunks to the damp earth and various flowers, there were too many scents to distinguish whatever it was that had caught my attention. Pongo's ears pricked, as his attention shifted to the same direction. So he had heard it too then?

'What is it?' Whip asked me.

'I need you to take Diego from me,' I said quietly, already crouching down so that I could lay my friend on the ground.

'Elodie?'

I fixed my eyes on the dense undergrowth of the woodland. Searching for something amongst the green. Something that could explain the prickling sensation on the back of my neck that was making me believe there was someone out there. A flash of colour flitted through the thicket.

'There's someone... there, in the woods,' I said. 'Someone's watching us.'

CHAPTER
ELEVEN

'Elodie!' I heard the warning in Whip's voice as I raced away from the road, but I didn't stop. Someone *was* there. Someone had been watching us. And Diego. I needed to know who. If whoever's behind this was responsible for the hex and chaos, then I had to find them. Fast.

My feet barely touched the ground as I headed into the undergrowth.

'Crap. Ow. Jeez—' Whoever thought vampires didn't feel pain was sorely mistaken. Sure, we heal fast enough, but that doesn't change the fact that having thousands of thorns and branches digging into you from every angle is less than pleasant. Add to that the fact that there was no way for me to build up any real speed, and the frustration was overwhelming.

'I can hear you!' I yelled. 'I can hear you! Just stop! You're not going to get away from me, you should know that!'

I sounded certain, but was I? This was Wraith Woods. The hunting ground and home of hundreds of werewolves. Sure, it could have been one of them, but if that was the case, why wouldn't they have just stopped and made themselves known? This person was running, which meant they were either guilty or afraid, and something told me this was definitely a case of the former.

I didn't know how deep this forest went, but it couldn't go on forever. Sooner or later, we'd come to the edge of the island, to the waterfront, where it was around a fifty-fifty chance of it being a soft sandy bay, or a damn steep cliff.

Ahead of me, feet crunched on twigs and grasses, the snaps reverberating in the quiet and sending birds flying into the sky. Whoever it was, they were heavy-footed, and while I'd never seen a werewolf run – in human or wolf form – I got the impression that this person, like me, was trudging their way through the undergrowth the best they could. Meaning they wouldn't be a pack member.

That thought was reinforced when we skirted the edge of the wolves village.

Wanting to know more about who I was up against, I drew in a lungful of air, trying to pick up a scent, but all I got was woodland and sea, the latter of which must have been closer than I thought, judging by the strength of its aroma.

'You need to give up!' I shouted. 'There's nowhere to go. You're not going to get away.'

The trees were thinning. I could see daylight

dappling through them up ahead. This was going to come to an end very soon. Whether it came out on cliffs or beach, at least I'd get a clear view of whoever I was chasing down. Or so I hoped. But when I finally broke through the undergrowth, my foot wobbled as I teetered on the strip of land in front of me.

'What the—?'

My breath hitched. I looked down, only to gasp and stumble back, stopping myself from toppling over the side. So much for lovely soft sands. This part of the woodland had brought me straight out onto a thirty-foot drop into deep, blue water that crashed into white foam against the rocks. Immortal or not, I didn't want to think about what would have happened had I slipped. If getting snagged on branches stung, then a fall down there... well, that would likely be on par with a dose of Macoy Belkin's mermaid venom.

Panting from frustration rather than exertion, I scanned my surroundings. There was a thin strip of grass bordering the top of the cliff, but nowhere the assailant could have gone. The ledge I was standing on was barely a foot wide, and it was the same as far as the eye could see. In fact, in some places, it was just trees, with no ledge at all. I was grateful I hadn't burst through there, or I would've gone straight over the edge. So where were they? Had they gone back into the wood? No, I would have heard, if not seen that, so what other options were there? Could they really have made that drop into the water? I couldn't tell what lay below the waves, whether it was deep enough to jump into, but did *they* know?

The disappointment stung as I stared out in front of me. There had to be a clue. Something I was missing. So what the hell was it?

A loud rustling in the wood behind sent a small flock of birds up into the sky, but I didn't need to turn around to know it wasn't who I'd been chasing. As Pongo sat down beside me, he tapped his paw on my foot, like he was in need of one of his buttons and let out two loud barks. As it happened, he didn't need the button for me to know that he was less than happy.

'I'm sorry, boy,' I said apologetically. 'I know you hate it when I run off and you can't keep up, but it was really important, I promise.'

He let out a low rumbling sound that was remarkably similar to a scoff. With a long sigh, I bent down and rubbed him behind his ears. His tail let out a reluctant wag.

I let out a long sigh. 'How about we jog back slowly,' I said. 'So you can keep up. Will that work?'

This time his tail wag was far more enthusiastic, though as I turned to move, I hesitated and looked back down at him.

'I'm not waiting for you if you decide to chase a chipmunk though. You understand?'

Two barks later, he didn't even wait before bolting off into the wood. So much for staying together.

CHAPTER

TWELVE

Thankfully, Pongo kept his word, and even though one very small and cute chipmunk did appear in a tree in front of us, Pongo continued jogging by my side. Of course, there was a fairly good chance he hadn't seen or heard it, and that was the only reason he didn't leave me, but I was hoping it was down to my excellent training.

By the time I returned to the area of road where we had cuffed Diego, both he and Whip were gone. So, following the sounds of the commotion, I headed further back up the road. The traffic jam was still firmly in place, though there were now two police cars, rather than one.

'Evergreen,' Alex said, walking across to me. 'Whip said you saw someone watching?'

'They got away,' I said, shooting Whip a look that conveyed my disappointment. 'I should've been faster. I should have had them.'

'Don't do that to yourself,' he said. 'Don't. You can't beat yourself up about it.'

'I'm just glad you're okay.' Whip's voice was almost a whisper as he sidled up beside me and placed his hand on my waist. It was only the second time he had touched me in a way that was so chaste yet intimate, and a thousand sparks rose up my skin. 'Would it really hurt you just to stay put now and then?'

'Yes,' I squeaked out. 'Yes, it would.'

Whip let out a laugh before dropping his hand, though the tingles remained a moment longer.

'I should get this traffic moving,' Alex said. I jolted. Somehow, I had forgotten he was still standing there. I cleared my throat in embarrassment, though my attention remained on Whip.

'You're taking Diego to the hospital, right? Did you get hold of Vincent?'

Whip nodded. 'He's going to meet me there, but you're going to have to go in the car with Alex or walk back to town. I can't risk having you in the police vehicle with Diego. I don't know the extent of the hex or how it can be transferred.'

'Does that mean it could be transferred onto you?'

'Unlikely,' he said. 'I'm not susceptible to much and I have my team tightly warded to protect them against a lot of magic. You, on the other hand... well, I'd really like it if, for once, you didn't put yourself in unnecessary danger.'

I didn't consider doing my job and holding people accountable to be unnecessary danger, and I was about to open my mouth to say as much, but then I noticed the deep worry lines on Whip's face.

'Yes, fine. Yes, I'll... I'll run back, though,' I said. 'Alex, is Pongo okay with you? He can't keep up with me if I go vamp speed, and I want to get back as soon as I can. I need to tell the others what's going on.' Given the length of our jog through the forest, Pongo would almost certainly use the journey as an opportunity to curl up and go to sleep.

'Sure.'

Pongo was sitting by my feet, and while he didn't understand everything that was going on, he looked up at me with a hint of annoyance, as if he knew he was about to be left behind again.

'I won't be long. I promise.' I crouched down beside him and ruffled his fur in a manner I knew he loved. Still, his doggy frown remained. 'I just need to go speak to Bobby and Chloe, alright? And I'll pick you up from the station. Which means you'll be able to see Josephina again.'

No matter how cross he was at not being with me, his tail beat involuntarily at the name of his best friend.

'Come on buddy,' Alex bent down and scooped Pongo up into his arms, like he was a tiny dainty puppy, rather than a sixty-pound fuzz-monster. 'You're gonna sit in the car while I sort out this traffic. Okay? And if you manage not to chew or go potty, maybe I'll find a treat for you at the station.'

I leant forward to open the car door for Alex. As my

hand touched the handle, a distant voice pricked my ears.

'People need to know. People need to know about us. People need to know.'

I turned to Whip.

'Is Diego still muttering?' I asked. 'Was he still talking to himself when you put him in the back of the car?'

'Muttering,' Whip tilted his head to the side. 'I don't think so. Why?'

I didn't respond. Instead, the car door forgotten, I moved over to Whip's truck, where Diego was slumped forward, his body over his legs, the effects of the cuffs still holding firm. He was absolutely silent, though that syrupy smell still remained.

Trying to block out the beeping horns, grumbling drivers, and all the other sounds, I listened again. Focusing. Desperate to catch wind of that voice again. Almost immediately, it met my ears. 'People need to know about us. People need to know.'

The words were growing stronger, as if the person talking was coming closer. And I wondered how on earth I had thought it had been Diego because the voice was a woman's. And she wasn't local. A European accent, and there was something scarily familiar about the intonation of those six words she continued to repeat.

'Elodie,' Whip said. 'What is it? What can you hear?'

My chest tightened, and the air clamped in my lungs, as I finally knew who I was listening to.

'It's Theodora,' I said, my hand flying up to my mouth as I covered my gasp. 'I think Theodora's been hexed too.'

THIRTEEN

My reflexive response to learning that another of my colleagues had likely been hexed was to ask Whip if he would give me a pair of runed handcuffs so I could get them on Theodora ASAP.

'The last thing you want is for her to cause another traffic buildup somewhere else, or worse,' I said. 'This could have easily ended in an accident.'

'If she is hexed, then you are not going anywhere near her,' Whip replied without even a pause to consider what I'd suggested. 'Did you not hear what I said about being susceptible to whatever's doing this?' he said.

'Did you not hear what I said about causing an accident? There are more people to think about on this island than me.'

He let out a low rumble, and for a second, I thought he was actually going to say that wasn't true, and that I was his main priority.

Did I want him to say that?

Thankfully, before it reached that, Alex stepped in.

'I can get there almost as fast as you could, if I shift,' he said, putting Pongo back on the ground. 'I'll be able to hear her, too in that form, so I'll be able to locate her easy enough.' From out of his pocket, he grabbed his car keys and threw them to me. 'Drive down and meet me,' he said, before looking at Whip. 'You okay to get the traffic sorted, boss?'

'I guess I'll have to be,' Whip replied, although it was humour, not malice in his voice. 'Just make sure you don't put yourself at risk. Our wards don't protect us against everything.'

'I'll keep an eye on Diego while you sort things out here,' I said, needing to be as useful as possible. 'Then, when it's clear, I'll drive down to you, Alex, so you can put Theodora in the car and take her to the hospital. If you're okay to hold until then.'

'Sounds like a plan.'

I don't know what I was expecting to happen, but without another word, he stripped off his T-shirt, revealing an obscenely chiselled set of abdominal muscles. I knew Alex had a good body. I could tell by the way his shirts stretched across his chest. But this... this was something else.

'I know.' He offered me a wink as a smirk rose on his lips. 'Impressive, right?'

I opened my mouth, not sure how I was going to respond, when Whip spoke instead.

'Alex, buddy. Any chance you'd like to do your job and stop flirting with my woman?' he said.

A grin flashed across Alex's face and I'm sure it would have made him look even more gorgeous, but I was already turning away to look at Whip.

'Your woman?' I said, raising my eyebrows.

As I caught his eyes, a bashful smirk rose on his lips, causing that dimple of his to reappear. 'We'll talk about that later,' he said. Good gods, this island and its men. They were going to be the death of me.

'Cuffs?' Alex said. He was now stripped to his boxers and putting his clothes on the back seat of his car. With the type of control I didn't know I possessed, I kept my attention glued to Pongo, as if my dog had suddenly become the most interesting animal in the entire world. I was not an ogler. And I definitely didn't ogle my male friends, when the man I was certain was more than a friend was standing right next to me.

'There you go,' Whip said, pulling out another set of runed cuffs from his bag, only, rather than handing them to Alex, the way I expected him to, he chucked them into the air so that they landed on the ground around two feet in front of Alex's feet.

My jaw dropped in surprise. Was Whip really that jealous of Alex's flirting? A split second later, the Alex I had known and spent time with was gone, and in his place was a fully grown male lion.

'Okay,' I said, my body reflexively moving away from him.

The golden hues of his mane were identical to the hair that he normally wore tied in a messy bun, and his eyes still held something of Alex's cheekiness. But the rest of him? That was one hundred per cent lion.

Pongo raced to hide behind my legs, but I couldn't look away. I had seen shifters before. Candice Rosso had insisted on having some of her photos taken in her red panda form. There was a family of goat shifters, who would often stroll into Weirdoughs in their animal form to collect their orders and eat both the bag and the pastry in one go. But I'd never seen someone shift into an apex predator.

He should have been terrifying, but instead, he was absolutely mesmerising. With a low rumbling growl that caused Pongo to whimper, his front legs bent as he lowered his head to the ground and scooped up the cuffs in his mouth and turned around.

'I take it that's your first time seeing him change,' Whip asked.

'Yup,' I said, my eyes still locked onto the patch of road where Alex had been standing in lion form only a moment ago, only he was long gone, having raced away between the beeping cars.

'Well, it never gets less incredible. Now, come on, we need to get this road sorted, so we can get to the hospital. And you can ring the others. I'm sure they'll want to meet us there.'

FOURTEEN

As soon as Whip got to sorting out the traffic jam, I'd rung Bobby, telling him he needed to get to the hospital ASAP. Then, after dropping the car with Alex – who was back in human form and fully dressed–so that he could put Theodora, whose hands had taken on the same bark-like texture as Diego's, in the back seat, Pongo and I'd walked the rest of the way back to town.

I wasn't wrong about my pooch being tired. He'd managed a short stretch by jogging behind me, but I could feel his exhaustion, just like he could feel my frustration at having to go slow, when I desperately wanted to check my friends were okay. So for the last mile, I carried him. After all, what was the point in having vampire strength if I couldn't carry my oversized dog now and then?

Still, I made sure I didn't vamp speed it. I'd learned

from past experiences that Pongo suffered from major motion sickness whenever I did.

So far, I'd been fortunate enough to avoid Ravens Hollow's hospital. If you could even call it that. The size of the building was a clear sign they didn't have much need for it on the island. The white brick building, with parking for just two cars, looked more like a small clinic than anything more; it was just a waiting area and a couple of rooms off it. I'd heard of expansion spells being used elsewhere on the island. Magic that could make what appeared to be a small, nondescript home on the outside a mansion when you stepped inside. And I half expected to find something like that when I stepped into the clinic, and was disappointed when it wasn't the case. It was just as small on the inside as it had looked, and the only two chairs were currently occupied by Dylan and Bobby.

'Elodie, thank God you're alright. I was about to give you a ring to see where you'd got to.'

Bobby wrapped his arms tightly around me, squeezing so tight I could barely get my breath in. Bobby had only ever hugged me once before, when I'd come around from the mermaid venom, and the fact he was doing it now didn't make me feel good. Just how bad were the others?

'Pongo needed carrying, that's all,' I said. 'Where's Chloe? Does she know what's happened?'

Dylan nodded. 'I spoke to her, but I didn't tell her the details. I didn't want to worry her too much. She just had ten minutes until her lacrosse match finished, so I suspect she'll be here any minute.'

'And what about family members? Has Lotty been told? And Theodora's family? Does she even have anyone on the island?'

While I knew that Diego was married to Carlotta – or Lotty, as her friends called her – I was embarrassed to say I knew next to nothing about Theodora's personal life.

'Lotty's in there with Diego,' Bobby answered. 'I've decided not to tell Theodora's family for now. They're all on the mainland, and they're not close. June will make contact if it comes to that.'

If it comes to that?

I was still plucking up the courage to ask just how bad it was when Chloe swept into the building.

'Where are they? Are they okay? I heard someone talking outside about hexes. That's not them, is it? They haven't been hexed, have they?'

I exchanged a look with the men, wondering who exactly should break the news to her, but as it happened, our unsubtle, non-verbal communication was all it took for her to know that the people outside *had* been talking about our friends.

'Oh god, no.'

Her knees buckled, and I was pretty sure she was about to faint, but before I could sweep in and catch her, Dylan was there, his arm around her waist, keeping her steady.

'Vincent's in there now with them,' he said. 'Whatever's happened, he'll be able to fix it.'

Chloe nodded, though her breaths remained staggered and shallow.

'What do they do?' I asked, wishing I had even a vague idea of what was going on behind those doors with Theodora and Diego. 'When someone's been hexed. What's the protocol?'

Bobby let out a long sigh. 'It's not quite that straightforward,' he said, wringing his hands as he spoke. 'There's a lot of complications that go into hexes.'

'Such as?'

He bit down on his bottom lip.

'It depends who cast the hex,' Dylan said, taking over the conversation. 'And what they used to cast it. Whether it was runes or spelled on the person or some kind of distance magic. Some hexes can be placed into potions, to make poisons of sorts. Others come from cursed objects. They have to identify what caused it before they can work out how to fix it.'

I nodded. That made sense. You need a diagnosis before you can figure out the treatment.

'So how long is that going to take?' I asked.

'I don't know,' Dylan replied. 'I mean, when I was a kid, we went to school with this warlock who used to practice hexing us all the time. His mum and dad pretty much always knew what he was up to, though, so we only had a near-miss once, and even then, it was sorted out in a couple of hours.'

'A couple of hours, right.' I let out a long breath. I could manage a couple more hours. I hoped.

'Of course, they had the advantage that they'd known exactly who had performed it,' Dylan said. 'It took out a fair bit of the guesswork.'

That was definitely less comforting, so I chose to push it to the back of my mind.

'I just don't understand why anyone would want to hex Diego and Theodora,' Chloe said, her voice wavering. She was clearly only just holding back tears, though Dylan had now led her over to one of the two plastic chairs and lowered her into it. 'I mean, if it was you or Bobby, maybe I'd get it,' she said, looking at me. 'You investigate things. But Diego? He takes photographs. And Theodora... she catches our typos. She formats the fonts, for crying out loud. I don't understand why someone would do this to them.'

I looked at Bobby, and I wasn't the only one. Both Dylan and Chloe had their eyes on our editor. Rather than reply immediately, he let out a sigh and chewed on his bottom lip.

'I think it's safe to say they weren't the intended targets,' he said.

'Meaning?' I asked.

'Meaning I think they were going after the paper as a whole. Someone wants to stop us from doing our job.'

CHAPTER

FIFTEEN

It was forty minutes later, after we had all taken our turn in the plastic chairs, pacing the small hallway, or stepping outside of the building altogether to give ourselves some air, when the doors opened and Whip stepped outside. A tall man with reddish-tinged hair followed him. I'd never seen him before, but he looked remarkably like Nyrah. Vincent, her brother. I already knew from Nyrah that he was the one in charge of growing the various plants that she had in her phenomenal courtyard. Plants I suspected they used in her salon, as well as in his role. If that was the case, then that was another overlap between tip and para magic.

'Are they all right?' Chloe said immediately, bouncing to her feet. 'Tell me they're okay, aren't they?'

You didn't need to be an expert at reading facial expressions to see from the look exchanged between Whip and Vincent that things were less than ideal.

'We can't isolate the source of the hex,' Vincent said.

'There's no runes on their bodies. No cursed amulets slipped into their pockets. And no trace of spells on them, either.'

'Is that good?' I asked.

The long sigh that reverberated from his lungs seemed to confirm it was the opposite of good, and when my gaze met Whip's, he lowered his eyes ever so slightly.

'Well, direct hexes are often more powerful,' Vincent continued. 'But at least then I'd know what counter-hex to create. At the minute, it's just guesswork. And the last thing I want to do is something that causes more harm than good. If I do that, it could be catastrophic.'

From the corner of the room, Chloe let out a stifled sob.

'So you're saying you know nothing?' Dylan replied. 'That can't be right.' There was a sharpness to his tone, though I knew he didn't mean it. He was just worried about Diego and Theodora. Not to mention Chloe.

'What we *do* know is that Diego seemed to get a much larger brunt of the magic than Theodora,' Vincent continued. 'This bark-like texture – that seemed to be the most severe symptom – has spread up to his elbow, while I have managed to maintain the spread to her hands.'

'What happens if it keeps spreading?' I said. I had only glimpsed Diego's hands, but they had seemed almost immobile. If that spread over his entire body, would he survive?

Whip and Vincents's silence felt like conformation of my worst fear.

'You mentioned they were both at the paper before?' Whip said, instead, unsubtly avoiding answering us.

Us four Oracle employees nodded simultaneously.

'I went to cover a lacrosse match,' Chloe said.

'I had a meeting with an advertiser,' Dylan added.

'Bobby and I went to Weirdoughs,' I said. 'Then I came to the station to talk to Alex—'

'While I stayed there and had food with June,' Bobby said. 'Which was where I still was when Elodie rang me. I'm assuming you're not suggesting one of us could be responsible?' he added, with just the slightest timbre to his tone. 'Because I would vouch for every one of my team. I've got the salt of the earth working for me, so if you're thinking of stirrin' stuff up, you should know, I ain't gonna let that slide.'

The first time I met Bobby, I had been struck by his paternal aura, which was unsurprising; his four grown-up daughters were his absolute pride and joy. And this wasn't the first time I had felt like the recipient of that warmth. Yet it caused a deep glow to spread through me. Not to mention a pang of guilt that served as a reminder to call my own father ASAP.

Before I'd moved, I'd promised him that even though I'd been on the other side of the planet, we'd still speak weekly, but while I'd been great with sending photos – mostly showing him how quickly Pongo was growing – I wasn't so great at remembering to ring. I needed to make more of an effort. After all, I was the only child he had, and I knew how hard it had been when my mother walked out of our life without a backwards glance. The last thing I would ever want him to feel was that I had done the same.

Whip shook his head. 'No. I'm not insinuating that at all, and I apologize if you thought I was. But the fact they were both at the paper when they were hexed means that was likely where it happened. Which means I can't let any of you back into the building until it's been checked thoroughly.'

Bobby's eyes widened.

'We've got the paper to put out tomorrow,' he said. 'Theodora sends it to the printers. They don't mind a delay, but 2 a.m. is the latest it can go to them. I haven't missed an edition of The Ravens Oracle in over one hundred and sixty years. I'll be damned if I'm going to be the editor when the first one gets missed.'

Whip nodded. 'I understand. I do. And that's the last thing I want either, but we need to make sure the place is secure first.'

'And how do we do that?' I asked.

'We need a witch who knows about hexes to check the place.'

'A witch that knows about hexes?' I was about to ask how long it would take us to find one, when the door swung open. Standing there was someone who had become a familiar face to me in Ravens Hollow. I might have even gone so far as to call her friend. She was definitely someone I had an enormous amount of respect for.

She was wearing a light turquoise summer dress and a variety of crystal rings on her fingers, while her jet black hair was currently in a long braid that draped over the front of her shoulder. Though her eyes were her most alluring feature. So dark it was impossible to see where the pupils ended and her irises began.

'So,' Nyrah said, letting out a sigh and rolling those jet-black eyes of hers, 'let me guess. You need my help. Again?'

SIXTEEN

Whip and Vincent told us that we needed to go home. There was nothing we would achieve by hanging around the hospital, and Whip insisted that he would ring us all once Nyrah had looked over the Oracle office and confirmed it was secure. Given that he was the law, technically speaking, it probably would've been a sensible idea to listen to him. But if he didn't know that my talent for not listening was even more well-practiced than my talent for sniffing out a story then there was a lot he had to learn about 'his woman,' to use his words.

Without need for conversation, the entire group of us walked silently out of the hospital.

'I think I have to go home,' Chloe said through a muffled sob. 'Though I'm not sure I'm in quite the right state to ride my bike. I rang Mick to pick me up, but he's busy.'

'I'll take you,' Dylan offered without a moment's

hesitation,. 'Then I'll ride your bike back to yours, too, so you don't have to walk in in the morning.'

It wasn't much of a walk from Chloe's to the paper at all, and unlike me, she didn't have to worry about sunlight wards running out. But from the watery smile she offered Dylan, it was clear how much she appreciated the offer.

'You'd do that for me?' she said.

A slight colour tinged his cheeks.

'Of course I would,' he replied.

Sometimes it was impossible to believe Chloe couldn't see how absolutely in love with her Dylan was, but now probably wasn't the right time to say anything.

'You don't have to worry about coming back to the paper,' Bobby said to Dylan. 'I'm sure you've got other places to be.'

Dylan scratched his temple. 'I should call that advertiser I walked out on earlier. She was looking at spending big bucks. Probably won't mention the reason I had to leave, though. Don't think she'd feel so confident investing if she knew we were the target of some crazy hex plan.'

Bobby nodded in understanding.

'You're right. Do what you can to placate them, but keep everything to yourself. We don't rumour monger, and we're not fans of gossip. We're not about to become it now. Okay?'

The island already had a gossip vlog. Prue Parsons was a local redheaded sea witch who was unscrupulous when it came to snatching a story and I knew firsthand what it was like to be on the end of one of her videos. Unlike several people I knew, including Chloe, I did not subscribe to her channel and refused to watch anything she posted, though I couldn't help but wonder how she kept people watching during times like this when there was next to nothing going on in Ravens Hollow. Though the paper was forced to print true, yet decidedly dull stories like Claudine Rosso's knitting just to fill the column inches, I was sure Prue didn't think twice about making stuff up to get the clicks.

'I'm not going to say a word,' Dylan replied. 'But you'll ring me if you find anything?'

'Of course I will.'

He turned his attention to Chloe. 'Come on, let's get you home. And we can stop at Weirdoughs on the way to pick up a slice of the key lime pie you love too.'

'Would that be okay?' she sniffed quietly.

'Of course it would.'

As the two of them walked away, Bobby turned to me.

'Take it there's no point asking you to go anywhere,' Bobby said to me.

I shook my head. 'Nope. You neither?'

'No. I've rung Raquel and June. They know I'm okay. But that's my paper. I need to be there.'

I understood; of course I did. I hadn't even been in Ravens Hollow a month and a half, and I couldn't imagine how I'd feel if something happened to the paper. An attack on the paper; it felt absurd. But it also made more sense than the idea that someone had deliberately targeted Diego and Theodora as individuals.

'I guess we should follow those two,' I said, nodding my head towards Whip and Nyrah who were already striding down the road in the direction of the Oracle.

Pongo kept the pace in front of us. The rest had given him a new burst of energy and I was sure he would have happily had a proper run. But my head was whirring with thoughts.

'Bobby,' I said, unsure if I was overstepping by even suggesting it. 'You... you don't think this could be the people you talked about in California? The mainland paper? The ones you were shouting at this morning.'

Bobby's gaze dropped to Pongo rather than meet mine.

'I don't know, in all truth,' he said. 'If you'd asked me a month ago, I'd have said no chance. But now, with this new person in charge... I don't know. I never imagined this. Never.'

'Theodora and Diego, they kept saying the same thing. Saying that people had to know. Would that make sense? Would there be something about the paper they wanted to make public?'

Once again, Bobby shook his head. 'Dunno. But that don't mean there isn't. That's the thing about this island. It's got all sorts of secrets, and it likes to keep them to itself, until they can be used by someone or something's advantage, that is.'

I nodded, as if I understood what he meant. But I wasn't entirely sure I did. Did Bobby mean the island had secrets, or that the people and paras on the island did? Could an island be a thinking, sentient being? Before I'd arrived here, I'd have said no, but only a few hours ago, I'd seen one of my closest friends turn into a bloody great lion.

We stood there, silence swelling between us, my mind constantly flitting between the state of Diego and Theodora to who would do something like that, to what secrets this island could possibly hold, though I didn't voice any more of my thoughts. Only when the sound of footsteps echoed from the staircase in front of us did I speak again.

'They're coming,' I said, looking at Bobby. 'Whip and Nyrah. They must be done, which means maybe they know how to cure them.'

When Bobby and I had first stopped chatting, I'd tried to see if I could catch anything Whip and Nyrah had been saying, but I hadn't been able to get a single word from inside the building. Given I'd heard Theodora nearly a mile away, I shouldn't have had any issues listening in, but I suspected Nyrah had placed a sound dampening spell over the office. I had to give it to her – it was sensible thinking, even if it was annoying as hell. But now they were outside, and I had no intention of holding back.

'So?' I said. 'What did you find?'

'Did you find any runes?' Bobby said, his impatience rivalling mine. 'That's what Vincent said it could be, right? Runes?'

With a slight sniff, Nyrah pressed her lips together and offered a tight smile.

'Perhaps we should just listen,' I whispered to him.

'Right,' he grimaced, apologetically. 'Sorry, you tell us.'

This time, Nyrah took a long breath in, like she didn't think we could last without interrupting her again, and only after a slight pause did she speak.

'There were no unusual runes drawn anywhere in the building,' she started.

'What does that—?' I clamped my mouth shut before I could continue. 'Sorry. Go on.'

'I used an incredibly powerful locator spell that would have drawn them out to me if they were there. But the only ones I found I've placed here over the years, for various things.'

'So what does that mean?' I said, my impatience once again getting the better of me. 'If there are no runes on the bodies, and no runes in the building...'

'Well, it means this wasn't a standard hex. It could've been done through some kind of hypnosis, perhaps. Or they could have touched something, breathed something in, eaten something...'

I got the feeling that we were no closer to finding answers than we had been in the hospital, and that feeling wasn't a good one.

'So what do we do now?' Bobby asked.

Rather than answering him, Nyrah looked at Whip. It was clear she was concerned about saying the next part, but the Chief Inspector offered her a slight nod, encouraging her to continue.

'I don't want to ask you this, but it's difficult for me to spot anything that could have caused the hex when I don't know what the place looks like ordinarily. I don't know if there's anything missing. Or more importantly, anything that isn't normally there. If it was just your office, Bobby,' she said almost apologetically, 'I'd probably see any differences. I've spent time in there, when I've done warding stuff. But the main area...? Diego's desk...? I mean, I've no idea what things did or didn't normally look like there.'

'And you want to see if we can spot anything. Something out of place,' I replied.

Nyrah nodded.

'But if you don't feel comfortable, we will think of something else,' Whip joined in. 'And you haven't been here that long, so you might not notice it.'

'I might be able to smell it though,' I said, remembering that syrupy sweetness that had clung to Diego when I'd found him.

'I suspected you might say that,' Whip replied, before glancing at Bobby. 'I understand completely if you don't want to do this, you know.'

Bobby groaned as he shook his head. 'You gonna say anything else daft, so we waste time out here gassing, or are we going to get in there and see what's what?'

I'd never been nervous about walking into the Ravens Hollow office before. Not really. Even when I wasn't exactly sure what to expect, early on, or when I was still learning the ropes – which I still was to some extent – I'd always looked forward to going in each morning. Now, though, as I followed behind Nyrah and Whip, anxiety rolled through me.

'If you're scared, and want to change your mind, no one's going to think any less of you,' Whip said gently. 'I sure as heck won't.'

I shook my head. 'No, I'm fine, I promise, but I was thinking...'

'About our date?' he said with a smirk. 'I know it's not exactly the ideal night for it.'

A chuckle left my lips. In all the commotion, I'd completely forgotten that I'd agreed to go on a date with Whip tonight. And he was right; it didn't feel like the most appropriate time to kickstart our relationship. But that wasn't what I'd been about to say.

'No,' I said. 'I was thinking earlier... about Diego getting a higher dose of the hex, you know? Maybe whoever did this knew he's a werewolf. That's why they upped the hex on him.'

'If it was about the paras strength, then Theodora would be the one who needed the biggest shot of the spell. Given her heritage and everything,' he replied.

'Her heritage?'

His eyes widened at me. 'You don't know what she is?'

I shook my head. 'No, she's never told me and I didn't want to pry.'

'Right. Yeah. That's probably the best thing. But believe me, if anyone needed the bigger dose, it would be Theodora.'

Theodora was a super powerful para? Well, that debunked my initial theory. So maybe they were given the same size hex, it just affected her less because she was something different. And no matter how I racked my brain, I couldn't for the life of me work out *what* that something could be.

There were some fairly sizable personalities in the office, but I'd always found Theodora to be a contradiction. She was the quietest of us, by a long way, always head down at her desk, rarely coming into the kitchen for snacks or drinks unless Chloe or Diego really pestered her. But at the same time, she had this flamboyance about her. She always dressed in the same style: plain T-shirts and colourful maxi skirts that looked like she was about to start flamenco dancing. I'd complimented her on them once, and she gave a small smile and a brief thanks, but I could tell something about it made her awkward, so I hadn't commented on them again.

Thoughts of Theodora and Diego held fast in my mind as we opened the office door, though rather than thinking about how they had been, I thought about their current state. Their limp bodies when the cuffs had gone on them. The absent looks in their eyes.

'Just stay next to me, Pongo,' I said, offering him a brief pat on the head. He might have been better trained, but there was no chance I trusted him to wait outside on his own. And at least if he was in my sight, I could stop him from doing anything silly.

'So, what do you think?' Nyrah asked. 'Is there anything that looks out of place? I guess their desks would be the best place to start.'

'Why don't I look at Diego's and you look at Theodora's?' I said to Bobby.

I'd spent a lot more time at Diego's desk, looking at photographs to go with stories and generally gossiping. I knew women in the workplace were supposed to be the chatty ones, but honestly, in every place I'd worked, it had always been the men who were the serial gossips. Although Diego never believed he actually was one.

Despite all the time I'd stood there talking to him, this was the first time I'd really paid attention to his desk. There was the large family photograph he kept next to his computer, and normally a couple of food wrappers, too. Again – I didn't know if it was a werewolf thing – but Diego ate *a lot*. So much that Chloe only ever brought out the banana cakes or muffins she baked when he was out taking photos. Otherwise, none would be left for everyone else.

As I stood there, I drew in a lungful of air, and it *smelled* like Diego. Like walks in grass covered fields and double-shot mochas from Weirdoughs. It was almost disappointing that I couldn't see anything out of place.

'Anything?' Whip asked, coming over to me.

I shook my head. 'No. I'm pretty sure all of this was here when we left.'

'Right. Well, maybe Bobby's having more luck over at Theodora's desk. He might spot something we've missed.'

'Right... right.'

A silence formed between us. A small flicker crossed his eyes.

'This definitely isn't the reunion I'd hoped for,' he said.

'No. It's not the best, is it?'

Despite my words, I couldn't help a smile grazing my lips, and the flutter that stirred within me, accompanied by a familiar tug. An urge to reach out, to wrap my hands around the back of his neck and kiss him.

I hadn't felt any effects of the sun for the past few weeks, not since Nyrah had placed her ward on me. But given past experiences, I wasn't expecting it to last beyond six months. And that didn't just refer to the sunlight ward either. It probably wasn't a great time to talk to her about getting them looked at, and as for whether the protection against Whip's siren charms were working, I already knew the answer was yes. I'd got angry at him today. Angry when he'd tried to stop me from going after that figure in the woods, or putting the cuffs on Theodora. And the anger could only happen when the ward was working. Which meant that desire I was feeling to run my hand through his hair and place my lips against his was coming from me.

I stepped back from Whip, preparing to go over to Theodora's desk and talk to Bobby, when I stopped.

'Pongo?' I looked around me, searching for the dog who had, only minutes ago, been at my heels. 'Pongo?'

My stomach lurched. I should've checked on him.

Finally, I caught a glimpse of his wagging tail near Dylan's desk. I darted over.

'Pongo, what did I say about staying close?'

I started to scold him, but the dog looked up at me, his brown muzzle white and glistening. My gaze dropped to the floor – to the large box that had been dropped there. A box that hadn't been there before we left.

'Guys?' I said, my voice trembling. 'You know what you said about the hex possibly being placed in food?'

Nyrah and Whip were suddenly at my side, their eyes locked on the same spot as mine. 'They weren't there before,' I whispered. A box of a dozen doughnuts lay spilled on the ground. Though not all of them remained now. I didn't know how many Theodora and Diego had had, but I was sure of one thing. Pongo had just eaten more than his fair share.

CHAPTER
EIGHTEEN

I t felt as though all the air had been sucked out of the room.

'Elodie, Bobby, you need to get out of here!' Nyrah was pushing me to the side away from the box of donuts that Pongo had just been helping himself to. 'If these have been imbued with the hex I don't want any of you near them. Then that includes you too, Whip.'

'Pongo,' I said, unable to focus on anything else. 'What do I do? I don't know what to do.'

'Elodie, it's going to be fine,' Whip took me by the hands and pulled me around so that I was looking at him. 'I promise. If it's the doughnuts, Nyrah will find it. I'll get you and Pongo home. We'll set him up in a room. Quarantine him.'

Quarantine him? My heart stuttered. I couldn't do that. I wouldn't.

'I was going to pop to the station to see Raquel,'

Bobby's voice broke my whirring thoughts. 'I'll tell her and Alex that you're occupied for the rest of the day.'

'Thank you,' Whip said, before turning back to me. 'Elodie, let's get you home. Just you and Pongo. Did you drive?'

I nodded. My little yellow Mini, Maureen, was parked behind the office.

'I'll drive, if you're alright with that.'

I nodded again, handing him the keys while I picked Pongo up into my arms. Suddenly it didn't matter how big he was, or how big he was going to get. He was my puppy and would always be my puppy.

My feet moved without any conscious effort as I slipped into the passenger seat with Pongo in my lap. It had been the first time we'd sat together in the car like that for a long time, and judging by the way his tail was wagging, he was perfectly content. Though when he lifted his head up to mine and his tongue lolled out of for one of his slobbery kisses, Whip reached across and stopped him.

'If the hex was in the donuts, you can't risk him getting any of the residue on you,' he said. 'Maybe it would be best if you put him in the back.' Rather than speaking, I offered Whip a look that said exactly how I felt about being separated from Pongo at that moment. Even if the separation was only as far as the back seat. Whip pressed his lips tightly together before relenting with a sigh. 'Fine, just be careful, okay?'

'I don't understand why someone would do this,' I

said. 'Not to Pongo, but full stop. Why would they try to hex the paper?'

Whip pressed his lips tightly together. 'I don't know. But don't worry. I *will* find the answer. I'll find out who did this.'

My little house wasn't far from the office, and a couple of minutes later, we were in the driveway. Before I could even get my belt off, Whip was out the driver's side, and opening my door for me.

'Thank you,' I said, as I climbed out, still refusing to let Pongo go, despite the way he was squirming. 'Thank you for getting me home. I'm not sure I could've coped with driving, not feeling the way I do right now.'

'You don't have to thank me. You know I'd do anything for you.' The way he spoke reminded me of how Dylan would talk to Chloe and I suddenly felt incredibly grateful that I hadn't stuck to my rule of swearing off men entirely since I'd moved here. If I'd done that, I had no idea how I'd be coping right now. As if he knew what I was thinking, he offered me a tiny dimpled smile. 'Come on, let's get inside.'

Once we were in the house, I headed to the kitchen and poured Pongo a large bowl of his favourite food. He sniffed at it, took a nibble – then stopped. My chest tightened.

'It doesn't mean anything,' Whip said quickly. 'We're not exactly sure how many of those doughnuts he ate. He might just be full up on sugar.'

I wanted to believe him, but I wasn't sure I could.

'Doughnuts would make sense,' I said. 'With Diego

having a higher dose and everything... he always eats more than his share. I bet he had several. I wonder how long it took to take effect. We might not have long. We need to be ready. Will your runed cuffs work on Pongo?'

The thought of my canine companion cuffed like he was a furry criminal caused a sob to stutter in my throat. It was almost as bad as locking him up in a room, to quarantine him, though thankfully, Whip hadn't mentioned that again. Clearly he knew what sort of response it could get. As the tears lodged themselves in my throat, Whip crossed the room and stood beside me.

'I know this is easy to say, but honestly, there's no point worrying. If it *was* the doughnuts, then Nyrah's already got them. She'll be working with Vincent to create an antidote, it'll all be good. I promise you.'

I *wanted* to believe him. Desperately.

'Well, from the doubt still in your eyes, at least we know the ward's still holding up on you. Right?'

'Right,' I said, offering only the weakest flicker of a smile.

'What have you eaten today?' Whip said suddenly, a change in his tone. 'Have you eaten anything?'

'I had my normal double-shot cappuccino from Weirdoughs.'

He arched a single eyebrow. 'So in terms of food, that would be a no, then.'

'I'm not that hungry,' I said. Any space in my stomach was consumed with fear. 'And I don't think I've got it in me to cook.'

'Well, how about you and Pongo curl up on the sofa,

put on some British soaps or whatever it is you like to watch, and I'll cook?'

This time, I couldn't help but choke out a laugh.

'Soaps?' I raised my eyebrows. 'I've never been much of a soap person.'

He frowned, looking generally confused by this comment. 'Really? I thought everyone in the UK was. What's that one called again? People loved it when I was over there. East Leavers?'

'*EastEnders*,' I corrected him, unable to stop a chuckle leaving my lips. 'You were in the UK?'

'Just for a few years. For work.'

What kind of work was that? I wanted to ask. The type of work he was doing now, helping a community or the one he'd been made immortal for – so he could change people's mind at the whim of the man who'd cursed him. Whatever Whip and I were, we weren't in a place where that was something I could question. And so I backtracked back to our previous topic. 'Maybe I would've been into soaps if I'd had time. But my job didn't really allow for that. Also, you don't have to cook for me.'

'I know I don't have to. But maybe I *want* to. I like cooking. And I haven't cooked for anyone in a while.'

'Well, you're not going to find much in the fridge, I'm afraid. And by much, I mean anything.' A flurry of embarrassment rippled through me. Now that I knew I could get my haemoglobin fix from Weirdoughs, I didn't even bother having blood bags in the fridge. If there was any food in there, it was almost certainly old and wilted, and the last thing I wanted was for Whip to see that.

'It's fine,' he said, flashing me a smile. 'I'll go to the shop and get some things. Do you want anything else while I'm there?'

'Vodka and Coke,' I said. 'Lots of vodka.'

He chuckled. 'I'll get the biggest bottle they've got,' he added, before glancing at Pongo, who was pawing at his bag for the buttons. Crouching down, I emptied them out and turned them over one by one so that he could use them. 'It doesn't look like there's any sign of the hex yet, but if you think he is – and I know you don't want to, but you need to – then place these on him.' He handed me one of the silvery cuffs he'd used on Theodora and Diego. 'He's only little, and these things are strong enough to bring down a Minotaur, so just one should work fine.'

It was possibly the first time someone had ever referred to Pongo as being small, let alone to a Minotaur being a real thing, but I was grateful. Cuffing one paw felt infinitely better than two.

As I nodded in agreement, a look of worry passed over Whip's face.

'Maybe it would be best if I stayed. We could order something in...'

I shook my head. 'No, it'll be fine. You won't be long, and I can hold him if I need to.'

He bit down on his bottom lip. 'If you can't do the cuffs, it would be better just to let him go. You don't need to hurt yourself trying to stop him from getting away.'

I lifted up my wrist and held it out to him. 'No pulse, remember? I'll be fine.'

As he reached the door, Pongo hit one of the buttons that I had finally finished sorting.

Bye

Whip looked from me to Pongo and back again.

'Smart dog,' he said before flashing me another smile. 'I'll be as fast as I can.' And with that, he disappeared.

CHAPTER
NINETEEN

I slumped down onto the sofa, letting out what felt like the heaviest sigh of my life.

'How are you feeling?' I said to Pongo. 'Can you tell me how you're feeling?'

We had several buttons, along with the sad one, to help Pongo identify how he was feeling. The most commonly used one was hungry, but there was also happy and tired and it was the latter of which he pressed then.

Tired

The words buzzed out.

'I get you, buddy. I feel the same,' I say.

Elodie sad, he pressed next.

A stray tear escaped down my cheek.

'More "worried",' I said to him. 'Not that we've learnt what that word is.'

A dull ache spread through my chest. Sometimes, when I looked at Pongo, I wondered how I had ever believed I loved my ex-Andy. What I felt for my best furry friend, was so much more than that. I got that it was a different type of love, of course, but I'd been going to marry Andy and spend the rest of my life with him, when I didn't even like his company that much. No matter how I was feeling, how stressed or overworked, he *never* tried to look after me the way Pongo did. So that was it, I decided. My new benchmark to measure all men by. Did they want to look after me as much as my dog did? My thoughts immediately went to Whip and how, at that moment, he was out shopping for food to cook me dinner. It definitely looked like he was meeting that requirement.

Swallowing back any potential tears, I tapped the seat of the sofa next to me and flashed Pongo a quick grin. 'Come on. You want to give me a cuddle?'

His eyes lit up in disbelief, before he tapped yet another button.

Happy

The slightest laugh escaped my lips. 'Well come on then,' I laughed. 'Get up here.'

Not needing to be told again, he jumped up next to me. I had tried to enforce a no-sofa rule – not because I didn't love cuddling with him (God knows I got plenty of that in bed every night), but it was only a two-person sofa. And I was well aware that sooner or later, if boundaries weren't put in place that two person sofa would become a one-dog throne, and I'd be forced onto the floor.

As Pongo got comfy, I pulled out my phone, and

acted on that pang of guilt that had struck earlier in the day, by calling my dad. The phone rang so many times, I was about to give up, when he finally picked up.

'Elodie.' His face flickered onto the screen, only to disappear again almost as quickly. 'Are you there? Hello, love. We're at the fy—'

'Sorry, Dad, I didn't hear what you said. Say it again?'

'We're at the— Can you h—' wherever he was, it was almost impossible to hear. If anything, from the echoiness of his tone to a noise remarkably like rushing water in the background, it sounded like he'd taken the call in the shower. Knowing Dad and Aggy, they'd probably grabbed a last minute cruise, and that was the reason reception was so bad. It wouldn't be the first time.

'Elodie dearest, is everything okay?'

My stepmother's voice came through far more clearly, but that wasn't entirely a surprise. I loved Aggy to bits, but that woman had a voice that could drown out an entire brass band. A million miles away from my actual mother Maria, whose voice I could barely remember now.

'Just wanted to tell you I love you,' I said.

'What was that, dear? You got cut off again.'

'I love you.'

'Sorry, what did you say?'

'I said I love you!' I shouted, loud enough that Pongo cocked his head at me in concern, but when their faces flicked back onto the screen, they were still crumpled in confusion.

It was pointless. I could see that conversation going

on for hours and getting absolutely nowhere. So I hung up the phone and sent him a text.

> Just wanted to say I love you

The response pinged back almost straight away.

> You too Elly Belly

'I'm sure they'll be somewhere else in a couple of days' time,' I said to Pongo. 'Hopefully, somewhere Dad can actually talk.'

Pongo's response to this was a long yawn and a slight stretch out. I hadn't been wrong about him wanting to make this sofa his own, but given what he'd been through, there was no way I was going to stop that happening now. I shuffled around, trying to make myself a little more room, when the doorbell rang.

'That can't be Whip, can it?' I said to Pongo, well aware he couldn't reply. Maybe if the buttons had been closer, he would have leant over and pushed one, but there was no way he was going to give up the sofa so soon after getting it. Still, it had been less than five minutes, and while I didn't know the full extent of Whip's para powers, superspeed shopping didn't feel likely.

Not sure I wanted to face anybody just yet, I took a sniff of the air, trying to identify the visitor by scent alone. There weren't many people, other than my colleagues at the paper, I could do that with, but when the sweet hint of honeysuckle struck, I knew exactly who it was.

'Alex?' I said as I opened the door. 'I wasn't expecting to see you. What are you doing here?'

'Evergreen, thank God you're okay. I heard about Pongo. Bobby just came to the station. I had to check you two were alright. Where's the big guy?'

At the sound of Alex's voice, Pongo lifted his head off the sofa. His ears twitched as he visibly debated the merits of getting off his seat to come and say hi to Alex, versus staying where he was. But, after a moment's deliberation he jumped down onto the floor, and trotted over, tail wagging.

'Hey, you,' Alex said, crouching down and rubbing under Pongo's chin in a manner that made my dog's eyes close in delight. 'You look okay, don't you? Or is that just because you can smell snacks?'

'Whip said it probably wasn't best to give him too much fuss, you know, in case there's still residue of the hex on him.'

Alex offered me a small smile.

'The wards they put on us police are pretty strong,' he said. 'Now, let me find you some of those treats.'

After standing up, he dug into his pocket and pulled out what appeared to be a pig's ear. Pongo's tail wagged so fast his whole body shimmied.

'Yeah, I know you like these,' he said. 'But I better check with your mum first. What do you say, Evergreen, can he have one?'

I think everyone knew there was no chance of me saying no.

'I suppose,' I said, unable to stop the smile that lifted my cheeks, as Alex crouched to give Pongo his treat.

'There you go,' Alex said, as Pongo proudly carried off his food to the kitchen. It was one of the few rules he actually stuck to. I had no doubt that when I stepped out of the living room to make calls, he was straight on the sofa. The dog hair gave that away. But he was good about where he ate.

'So how are you holding up? Pongo looks okay,' Alex said, 'but how are you?'

'Oh, I'm a wreck,' I said. 'Honestly, if Whip hadn't brought me back, I would've probably collapsed outside the paper and cried the entire evening.'

Alex offered me a sympathetic smile.

'Whip's a good guy, but I don't believe that for a second. You're way too tough. And so is that dog of yours. He's going to be fine. You know that, right? Him, Diego, Theodora, they're going to be fine. And then we – or, knowing you, probably you and Bobby – will find out who's doing this. And they'll have to pay for their crimes.'

I nodded. 'Thank you. And thank you for coming over. You really didn't have to.'

He shrugged. 'I just wanted to check you're alright. Didn't want you to be on your own. You know, if you need company, someone to sleep on the sofa or anything. And this is not me hitting on you. After earlier today, I wouldn't make that mistake. Well, not while Whip's in town,' he added with a grin.

A lump formed in my throat. He really was so sweet. And, other than Chloe, he was probably my best friend on the island.

'Thank you,' I said. 'That's really sweet. But actually... that won't be necessary.'

'Are you sure? I really don't mind—'

I opened my mouth, not sure why I felt so nervous about telling him that Whip had offered to stay instead, only for the very subject of conversation to appear behind us.

'Alex, what are you doing here?' Whip asked. 'Has something happened at the station?'

TWENTY

I was not the type of woman who found herself embroiled in love triangles. I barely found myself embroiled in relationships. And what I was experiencing now wasn't that. Not exactly. After all, Alex and I were just friends. We were *very definitely* just friends. He had just reinforced that was the only reason he had offered to crash at mine for that night.

But something about the way Whip's eyes moved between us made me think he wasn't quite convinced

'Hey, boss,' Alex said. 'Should've guessed I'd find you here.' He glanced down at the large tote bags in Whip's hands. 'Been doing some shopping?'

'Just sorting dinner,' Whip replied. 'Are you okay? What are you doing here? There hasn't been another hex, has there? You should have rung me.'

I could have been wrong, but it looked as though the tops of Alex's cheeks turned ever so slightly pink at the question.

'No, no more hexing,' he replied. 'At least, not that I know of. I was just checking on Evergreen. Didn't want her to be alone. You know, after what happened to Pongo. But like I said, I should have guessed you'd be here.' He turned to look at me. 'If this one's cooking for you, you're in for a treat, believe me. And if there are any leftovers I want first dibs.' He flashed me a smile and I wasn't sure why I felt a pang of guilt. We were all friends, would there really be anything wrong with him staying for dinner too? But then, tonight was meant to be my first date with Whip. Asking Alex to stay didn't seem right.

'Sure thing,' I said, instead. 'And thank you for Pongo's snacks.'

'Any time,' he grinned, before twisting back to look at Whip. 'Have a good night then, boss. And don't worry about the station. I've got it covered.'

'Got it. Thanks, buddy. And thanks for checking in on Elodie. I appreciate it.'

As Alex disappeared down the drive, Whip stepped towards me. 'Pongo still doing okay?'

'Yeah. He's just eating the pig's ear or trotters, or whatever it is Alex brought him.'

'Sounds appetising,' Whip chuckled. 'But, while we're talking about food, I forgot to ask what you ate before you left. So I picked up things for a few options. I thought I'd do a paella. Could do seafood, chicken, or veggie. Whatever you fancy.'

'Really, Whip, you don't have to. We could just get a takeaway.'

He scoffed. 'Our first date has already been derailed enough, don't you think? Now, which one?'

I contemplated the options before replying. 'Seafood,' I said. 'If that's okay?'

'Course it is. Sit down, I'll grab you a vodka and coke, and get to work in the kitchen.'

THIS WASN'T the first time in my life a man had cooked for me. Andy used to do dinner three times a week, but it was always chicken and rice or boiled potatoes, without fail. Even if he was feeling bold, confident that he hadn't had an IBS flare-up in some time, all he'd do was push the boat out with a lemon-and-black-pepper dressing.

But the smells coming from my kitchen were absolutely divine. I had asked if I could help, and every time, he had told me to go and sit down. So, not wanting to interfere, I used the opportunity to message my best friend.

Donna – my former editor-in-chief back in London – was still my go-to person to talk to about life. It was substantially harder now, with the time difference and everything. But given that it was early evening here, I was pretty sure that if she wasn't already awake, she would be within the next hour or so.

As it happened, I'd barely hit send when my phone started ringing.

'What the hell? What's going on?' Donna's panic resonated down the line.

For the next ten minutes, I filled her in on everything – from Diego and our first knowledge of the hex, right up to Pongo eating the doughnuts and Whip making me dinner.

'Has he got any suspects?' she asked. 'Any people he thinks might be behind it?'

I shrugged, even though she couldn't see it. 'I don't know. It feels like an attack on the whole paper and there's someone on the mainland that Bobby was arguing with this morning, because he won't let them buy us out. But I can't help wondering... what if it's about *me*?'

'About you?' she said sharply.

I nodded, even though again, she couldn't see it.

I lowered my voice to a near whisper. It was a theory I probably needed to share with Whip at some point, but I wasn't quite ready to do that.

'The Guardians are bound to have found out where I am by now. What if this was sent for me? What if I was the person they meant to hex? And that's not all, there was someone on the roadside when we found Diego. Someone watching.'

'You think that was the person who placed the hex?'

'It would make sense,' I said. 'They knew where we'd be heading, after all. Maybe they were hoping I'd be the one to find Diego, and they could grab me before the police got involved.'

On the other end of the line, Donna let out a long breath.

'Maybe,' she said carefully. 'But how would they

know you'd even go there? It should have been the police who reached him first, right?'

I'd already told her how I'd got out of the car and run to beat the traffic. Would a Guardian know me well enough to know I'd do that? It's unlikely they'd have predicted I'd be in the car with Whip. But I still couldn't shake the feeling that this was something to do with me. Like Chloe had said, if anyone was going to make enemies at the paper it would be Bobby and me.

'There have to be other suspects too, right?' Donna continued, breaking my stream of thoughts. 'You can't jump to that. I *know* you. You're feeling guilty, even though there's nothing to feel guilty about.'

Was that true? Did I feel guilty about things that weren't my fault? I'd definitely felt guilty a long time for the way my mother had abandoned dad and I, but I'd been a child then. As soon as I'd been old enough to realise that she'd been the one with responsibility in the situation, that guilt had changed to anger.

'How's Pongo?' Donna said, redirecting the conversation to the present.

Pongo had moved from the sofa into the kitchen with Whip—most likely hoping to be given a tasty tidbit while Whip was cooking. Very standard Pongo behaviour. And from what I could tell, there was no evidence of the bark-like texture that had replaced the others' skin. But it was difficult to tell, given he was covered in fur and everything.

'He seems okay,' I said. 'I'm not sure how hex symptoms might appear in a dog versus a person, though.'

'You said Diego and Theodora's skin changed, right? And they were walking somewhere. Surely he'd be doing the same. How long has it been since he ate the doughnuts?'

'I'm not sure exactly,' I admitted.

I checked my watch. It had been around fifty minutes since Pongo had eaten his. So did that mean we were still in the danger window? Maybe. But if we got to two, maybe three hours – I'd feel a little more at ease.

'Look, I need to jump in the shower before work,' Donna said. 'But if there's any change, ring me, okay? If you need me to hunt down the best damn hex specialist in London, I'll do it, you know that.'

I did, just like I knew she'd jump on a plane and fly out to me in a heartbeat if I asked her. Not that I would.

'I should probably go, too,' I said. 'I don't know how long dinner's going to take, and I probably shouldn't be on the phone the whole time he's here. You know, bad manners and all that.'

'Just keep me updated?'

'Of course I will.'

A moment later, the call ended, and Whip appeared in the doorway wearing an apron. Had that always been in the kitchen? Embarrassingly, I wouldn't know, having only looked in half of the cupboards. Still, he looked surprisingly good in it. But then, he could have worn a bin bag and still looked impeccable.

'How are you feeling?' he asked. 'I'm guessing that was Donna on the phone. Did she say anything helpful?'

'It was just good to get it out,' I said truthfully. He

nodded in understanding. A man who cooked and knew when you needed to speak to your best friend? He really was proving to be the total package.

'Well, Pongo's still doing okay. And he seems to have a love of paella too.'

A choked laugh rattled out of my throat.

'I think you'll find he has a love of food in general.'

'Well, that's probably it. Anyway, that's my part done now—just needs to simmer a bit. I was going to check outside, give Raquel and Alex a ring, see if there've been any updates.'

'Sure,' I said. 'And... you really don't need to stay here with me.'

He offered me a withering glare.

'After I've just made all that food, you think I'm going to leave without eating any? No chance.'

After finishing his call with the station, Whip came back into the house, and disappeared into the kitchen. Ten minutes later, he was standing in the doorway, a napkin over his arm and two plates in his hand.

'Dinner,' he said, a smile twisting his lips, 'is served.'

CHAPTER
TWENTY-ONE

I leant back in the chair and rested my hand on my belly. My plate was utterly empty. There would be no leftovers for Alex, or anyone else for that matter.

'That was incredible,' I said, still unable to believe that someone had whipped up a meal like that, in a kitchen where I had barely made more than a cheese toastie. 'Where did you learn to cook?'

'It's not that impressive really,' Whip said with a shrug. 'When you're immortal, you've got plenty of time on your hands. It's the immortals who can't cook you need to worry about. I mean... what *are* they doing with all their time?' His smirk revealed that adorable dimple that always made my heart skitter. For someone who could look so imposing, that dimple softened him. It was like a little secret gesture that was only kept for me. I hoped.

It's weird, really. The number of books and films I've

watched where the innocent, naïve young woman falls in love with the morally grey immortal of unknown age had always made me a little dubious. I mean, you'd be able to tell, right? Even if they were in the body of a hot twenty-something, you'd *surely* be able to tell if they were, like, three hundred years old.

That's what I'd thought, at least.

But looking at Whip, it was impossible to believe he was a day over thirty. He didn't smile like someone who'd seen centuries. He didn't carry that weight in his eyes. The question of actually asking him floated in the back of my mind, but I didn't dare. The last thing I wanted to find out was that the guy I was crushing on had been around when the pyramids were built.

'You look like you're thinking very intently,' Whip said, drawing me out of my thoughts. 'Anything I should know about?'

I shook my head. 'No. Nothing really.' I lied.

Pongo was already snoring away. We had now passed the two-hour point. Without doubt, Diego and Theodora were feeling the effects of the hex by this point, and it should have made me relax, but as far as I was aware, Pongo wasn't a para. He was just a normal dog. And who knew how long it would take for the effects to take hold on someone, or something without magic? Still, it was good to see him relaxed, and it meant that one of us was going to get some rest – because there was no way I'd manage it, not with the worry still burning in my chest. The thought of having to stay awake caused a wide yawn to escape.

'Why don't you head to bed,' Whip said, reaching over and putting his hand on my arm. 'I'll wash up, then sleep on the sofa, if that's alright with you.'

'You don't need to do that.'

'It makes sense, from a police point of view, you know. If something happens to Pongo, I can alert the others.'

His hands shifted so that our fingers interlocked on the top of the table.

'So, it's official work to spend the night on my sofa?'

'Oh yes,' he said, his dimple sliding back into view, 'because if it *wasn't* official work, then it wouldn't be your sofa I'd be spending the night on down here.'

I felt myself move closer to him, almost unconsciously.

'I thought about you all the time I was away,' he said, his voice a low rumble that caused my entire body to shudder in the best possible way. 'I'm sorry, I feel like I should have rung you. I just didn't want to pester you, you know? I didn't want to be overbearing. I wanted to give you some space.'

'And now that you're back?'

He was so close I could feel the heat radiating off him. The tension stretched between us like a thread pulled taut.

'Now... space is the last thing that's on my mind. God, when I saw you and Alex together when I got back—'

'Alex and I are just friends,' I said.

'I know. I do, but this is new for me...wanting someone the way I want you, it's not normal for me.'

'Well, that makes two of us.'

Before he could say any more, or I could question what I was about to do, I leaned in and planted a kiss on his lips.

I thought sparks were a thing of movies. Fiction spouted by books and films to make us feel like we were missing something in our lives. But these sparks were very much real and spread through every part of me. Maybe it was because I was a para now, or because I had been imagining this moment since the first time I saw him, but I could feel everything about the moment. His heartbeat. His hands around the back of my neck. His reluctance to stop kissing, as I drew myself away from him.

'That was... something,' he said quietly. His eyes glinted as they stared into mine.

That was one way of putting it.

'Still sleeping on the sofa?' I asked.

'Tonight I am.' He grinned. 'After that... we should probably wait and see.'

TWENTY-TWO

When I woke up the next morning, it was to the smell of fresh coffee and the sound of someone downstairs. My heart throbbed. Whip really had stayed all night on the sofa.

I rolled over to find Pongo in his normal place next to me on the bed, sitting up expectedly, like he had been waiting for me to wake.

'You look good,' I said, ruffling his fur. 'Do you feel good?' His buttons were still downstairs, yet I took his wagging tail as a yes. 'Come on, we should go and see Whip.'

Downstairs, Whip had shed his black shirt and was wearing a white vest with his dark jeans, though it was a tough call as to whether I locked my attention on the curves of his biceps, or the cup in his hand.

'I did a Weirdoughs run,' he said. 'Omar said you were off the double shots and back on the negatives, so if it's wrong, blame him.'

Omar. Somehow, I'd been in Ravens Hollow all this time and visited Weirdoughs at least once a day, but hadn't learnt the owner's name until now. Schoolgirl error.

I took a sip of the coffee. Perfect.

'Have I told you that you're incredible?' I sighed as I looked at Whip.

'Oh, I'm not. But you make me want to be.' There was absolute sincerity in his voice, and I wanted nothing more than to see if morning kisses were just as amazing as evening ones. But before I could, he carried on talking.

'Pongo seems alright,' he said, crouching down and stroking gently behind the dogs ears. 'No sign of anything happening to his skin. I thought at one point in the night he was going to get up and vanish, but turns out there was just a chipmunk in the garden he wanted to chase.'

'You waited up all night? Have you had any sleep?'

'I'm fine. I really don't need that much.'

The question of why crossed my mind. I was the vampire, and yet somehow he needed less rest than me. Then again, maybe he was just saying that, and the moment he left here, he'd go to his flat above the office and take a nap.

'So, what does that mean?' I asked. 'Does it mean it wasn't the doughnuts?'

Whip shrugged. 'I don't know. Could be they were designed to work on magical creatures only, so they had no effect on Pongo. We'll just have to wait and see what Nyrah comes back with.'

A silence settled between us, not entirely comfortable, but not quite awkward either. I wasn't the only one feeling it. We'd kissed once more after dinner, when Whip had walked me upstairs and said goodnight, but now that the new day had arrived... it was like we weren't sure what the rules were anymore.

'Thank you for last night,' I said quietly. 'For staying with me. For cooking dinner and...'

'And...?' he said, the smile glinting in his eyes.

'And I'd like to do it again. Though preferably under less traumatic circumstances.'

He chuckled in a way that made my knees go weak, then slipped his hand around my waist, and pulled me in.

'I'd like that too,' he said, before lowering his head and letting his lips meet mine.

I didn't know it was possible, but somehow morning kisses weren't just as good as the nighttime ones. They were even better. I pushed myself on to my tiptoes, pressing myself deeper into the kiss, wondering why on earth I'd let him sleep on the sofa. And how the hell I'd coped with such bland kisses my entire life until this point. It was even more criminal than all the unseasoned chicken I'd eaten. No, this was now the benchmark for every kiss I would ever have, and I had no intention of stopping anytime soon.

Unfortunately, someone had a different idea.

Out. Out. Out.

Pongo's button buzzed through from the living room.

I pulled away from Whip but kept my hand wrapped around his neck, as I looked at my dog.

'Really?' I arched an arrow. 'The backdoor is open. You could go out any time you wanted.'

But rather than moving, Pongo stamped his foot on the button again.

Out.

With a reluctant sigh, I dropped my hand and stepped back away from Whip.

'I guess he wants me to go with him,' I said. 'Sorry.'

Whip grinned, slipping his hand into mine. 'It's fine. I should leave now too, or I'm never going to get out of here.'

'I wouldn't have a problem with that,' I said, unable to stop myself from smiling.

He leant back into me, and the warmth of his breath caused a shiver to run down my spine.

'Yeah, but it would mean you wouldn't get any new articles written. And someone else might beat you to a scoop.'

Damn it, that man knew how to play me perfectly. Immediately, I stepped backwards.

'Okay. On second thought, you should definitely get going,' I said, pressing my hands on his chest. 'The sooner the better, actually. You know, I have a job to do, and you are very distracting.

'Is that right?'

'It is.'

The dimple was firmly in place as he looked at me,

shook his head and chuckled, before picking up his shirt from the back of the chair.

'I'll see you later, Elodie,' he said, turning to the door. 'Try not to get into any trouble before then. Please.'

TWENTY-THREE

As much as I wanted to get to the office, I didn't leave straight after Whip. My first job was to message Donna and tell her that firstly, Pongo was alright, and second, Whip and I had kissed. Several times. I was hoping she would respond, but it wasn't a surprise when the message went unread.

After getting out of the shower, I was unsure whether I wanted to drive or walk. It was a beautiful morning, and driving really didn't save that much time, but if we got a scoop, then I'd need to get to wherever it was on the island as quickly as possible. Which was why I made the decision to take the Mini. So, with Pongo's buttons and my laptop in my bag, I opened the car door, ready to go. But before I could get inside, I was stopped by a voice.

'Elodie? Are you okay?'

I turned around and, much to my surprise, found a woman standing on my driveway.

Amira. That was her name. I didn't know if she had a

surname. I'd bumped into her several times since moving to Ravens Hollow, though I had no real idea what she did, or what type of para she was, though her large pointed ears that left her head at a forty-five degree angle indicated she was a fae of some sort. The last time I'd seen her, I could've sworn her eyes were hazel. This time, they were a much lighter peridot, and though her face was crazily wrinkleless, there was clear concern in her expression.

'Sorry,' she said, 'I didn't mean to interrupt. I'd heard something terrible had happened to people at the paper. That people there were being hexed, and, well... I just wanted to check that you were okay.'

'Oh. Right...' Should I have been concerned that a random fae knew where I lived on the island and turned up at my house without any sort of invitation? I wasn't entirely sure. Yes, I had spoken to Amira before, but only ever in passing. Then again, this was a small town. I suspected half the people here probably knew where I lived. At least the ones who could be bothered to care.

'Yes, yes, I'm fine,' I said, walking towards her, a knot of uncertainty building in my stomach. 'Sorry, how did you find out about the hexes?'

I stared at her, eyebrows raised as I awaited an answer, and she blushed.

'I overheard Nyrah talking to her brother about it. I know it was terrible of me to eavesdrop, but it wasn't deliberate.'

'Nyrah was talking about it at work?' I said. I'd always pegged Nyrah as incredibly professional. Talking where her customers could overhear was not something I'd ever imagined her doing.

'Oh, the shop wasn't open,' Amira said hurriedly. 'I work there. Just part time. Nails and facials mostly. No magic. Just the beauty side of things. You must think me awfully nosy, but I was just worried about you. You know, being so new to the island and everything, and not knowing how things work. I imagine it must've been scary for you to deal with things like that. Not that it gets much easier when you've been in the para world for longer.'

The woman really was a puzzle to me. More than once, she'd mentioned knowing what it was like to be new to this life, although as far as I was aware, fae were born; you couldn't be turned into one. So maybe she just meant Ravens Hollow? There was also something about her choice of words. 'Awfully nosey' sounded British, yet her accent was definitely American. Where in America, I couldn't place. But then that was more a me issue than her. Maybe she was just a lonely old woman who needed some company and had decided she wanted to form a connection with me. Was it ideal? Possibly not, given I knew nothing about her, but was it the worst thing in the world? Probably not.

'Well, thank you,' I said. 'Thank you for checking on me. But yes, I'm fine.'

She nodded, looking visibly relieved by that. And she remained exactly where she was.

'Sorry,' I said, 'I don't mean to be rude, but I kind of need to get to work.'

'Of course. Of course, sorry,' she said quickly. 'I'll let you get on. So glad you're alright, Elodie. I'm sure your father would've been devastated if anything had happened to you.'

'I'm sure you're right,' I said. 'Thank you.'

With that, I got into the car. Pongo climbed in, and I switched on the engine, watching in the rearview mirror as she walked away.

Only as I pulled out of the driveway, and saw Amira still standing there on the side of the road, did her choice of wording strike me as odd. Wouldn't most people have said *family*, not just *father*?

Then again, maybe I was just being paranoid.

TWENTY-FOUR

It was with a strange flutter in my chest that I walked back into the office, and it was only partially to do with the hexes. On one hand, Chloe would be desperate to know about the progression in my relationship with Whip, and I wanted to tell her. But at the same time, it didn't seem appropriate. Not while the fates of Diego and Theodora were still unknown. Not to mention how the rest of us that worked at the paper could still be under a very real threat, and as far as I was aware, we had no idea where it was coming from.

Unusually, I was the last one in the office. Normally, even when there wasn't much to write about, I was early – painfully early – but then again, I didn't normally spend the night panicking that my dog was the latest victim of a malicious attack. Nor did I normally have Whip bringing me my coffee.

'Elodie!' Chloe said, coming over and squeezing me tight in a hug. I had got used to the hugs, just like I had got used to the way she would also ask you countless questions in a row without giving you time to answer. They were little things that made her so endearing. 'Thank goodness Pongo's alright. Is he alright? Are you alright? He looks alright, but have there been any signs? Bobby told us what happened last night. Why didn't you ring me? You know you can ring me right? Any time?'

'He's alright,' I said, deciding to pick the main question to answer. 'I think. We're pretty sure that if the hex was going to affect him, it would've done so by now.'

'Thank goodness,' she nodded, letting out a relieved sigh before dropping to the ground and wrapping her arms around the pooch's neck. Given all the licks he'd given me in the morning, I had stopped worrying about any form of hex residue in his slobber. 'I wonder if there's been any news about Diego and Theodora yet? Do you think Bobby's called Whip? Or do you think he'll come here?'

'I'm not sure,' I said. 'Though Whip didn't have any more news this morning when he left,' I replied.

Her eyes widened.

'Whip stayed? You mean at your house? Whip stayed the night with you?'

Her jaw was hanging so low it was comical.

'He stayed because of Pongo,' I said quickly. 'On the sofa.'

While she managed to close her mouth, Chloe's eyes shifted from bulging to narrow as a small twist curled at the corner of her lips.

'Elodie Evergreen... did something happen between you two? You have to tell me right now.'

There was only one question this time, meaning I couldn't pick which one to answer and pretend I hadn't heard the rest. I cast a glance sideways. Bobby's office door was closed, which I took as a sign that he was in there. Dylan was already fielding phone calls at his desk. Neither of them were listening.

'We may have kissed,' I said, unable to suppress the smile on my lips. 'A few times.'

'Eek!' Chloe squealed, grabbing my arms and squeezing tightly. 'Oh, my God! Tell me everything!'

Well aware that neither of us would be getting any work done until she was satisfied I had filled her in on all my gossip, I nodded over to my desk and took a seat, at which point she pulled her chair over to me.

'There's really not much to tell,' I said, fairly certain she was expecting all sorts of sordid details. 'He cooked me dinner, we kissed, then he walked me upstairs to my bedroom, like a gentleman, and we kissed again, before he went to sleep on the sofa.'

'And this morning?' she pressed. 'You said he was there this morning.'

'He was. When I came down, he'd brought me coffee from Weirdoughs. And... we may have kissed again.'

'That is absolutely not "not much to tell". That's loads to tell! So is that it? Are you two an item now? Are you Whip's girlfriend?'

'I don't know,' I said. 'He did call me "his woman," in front of Alex yesterday.'

She let out a sigh before shaking her head.

'That's so romantic, although, poor Alex must be heartbroken. Half the single women in town will still be glad he's available.'

'Alex will not be heartbroken,' I said. 'He and I are just friends.' I should probably message him and tell him Pongo was okay. Just in case he hadn't seen Whip yet.

'When are you seeing him next?' Chloe propped up her chin on her hands as she spoke. 'Whip, that is.'

'I'm not sure,' I said truthfully. 'He's kind of got more important things to think about right now.'

'Of course.' The smile that had been lighting up her face faded, and a heavy silence settled between us. 'I was drawing up a list last night,' straightening up as she spoke.

'A list?'

'People who might have something against the paper. Or against one of us.'

It was good thinking, and had I been in my right mind, I would have probably done the same thing. But then, it wasn't like I knew enough people on the island to make a comprehensive list, anyway.

'Did you come up with many?'

'A few,' she admitted. 'I mean, it's not like some of our articles haven't ruffled feathers, but to go to this extreme? It just doesn't feel like something someone from Ravens Hollow would do.'

Again, I felt it in my gut. The possibility that it was The Guardians behind all this, to punish me for what I had done. And my friends had gotten caught in the crossfire, simply because they worked at the same place I did.

It was something I needed to bring up with Chloe. I knew that. Yet, before I could, her phone let out a strange chiming sound.

'What's that?' I asked. 'Is that an alarm?'

'Notifications,' she said, pulling her phone from her pocket. 'The Scoop's got a new vlog post out.'

'You get notifications from The Scoop?'

I couldn't help the indignation in my voice. The online excuse for journalism was the reason photos of me in a lion onesie had been circulating Ravens Hollow before I'd even stepped foot on the island. Prue was unscrupulous and venomous, and stood for everything good journalism was not.

'I just keep an eye on it,' Chloe said. 'Never know what bit of vindictive rubbish she's going to start spreading. You know that.'

She clicked open the video, sitting back in her chair. It had barely started playing when her hand flew up to her mouth.

'You have to be kidding,' she hissed.

TWENTY-FIVE

The four of us were standing in Bobby's office watching the video. Sort of. Chloe had dragged Dylan in with us, even though he was still answering messages on his phone.

'It makes perfect sense.' Chloe pointed at her phone, which was now lying face up on Bobby's desk. The video clip was playing on repeat. Not that we needed it to. We all knew what it showed; Diego, walking mindlessly down the centre of the road, and me trying to stop him.

'She's had nothing to post for days. It's been dead slow this week and last. I bet she hexed them just so she'd have a story.'

Bobby's brow furrowed. 'That's a big leap, Chloe,' he said.

'Is it?' she shot back. 'Then why was she there? She's a sea witch. She lives nowhere near there. What business does she have hanging around on the side of the road in Wraith Woods?'

'She is a sea witch,' I added, the realisation clicking into place. 'And whoever I chased through the undergrowth, they must have gone into the water after the cliff. There was nowhere else for them to go. I thought it was impossible, that they wouldn't survive the fall. But Prue? She could've survived it.'

Bobby let out a long sigh.

'Not that I'm taking sides here,' Dylan said, finally putting his own phone down to talk to us, 'but advertisers like there to be news. Papers sell more when there's something people want to read. Normally something juicy. I know she's got a vlog, not a paper, but I'd bet her advertisers aren't thrilled about paying for screen space when she's getting zero views.'

Bobby sucked in a deep breath. 'Let me have a ring around. See what I can find out.'

'No.' Chloe placed her hands on her hips and stared at the boss with a kind of defiance I'd never seen from her before. 'That'll take ages and she'll slip away. She's not getting away with this.'

'Chloe, I don't want you doing something silly here,' Bobby warned.

I would've expected the Fae to wilt under that tone. But she didn't. Instead, she straightened her spine so that she stood a good inch taller.

'Whether she hexed them or not, she knew something. She had some idea what was going on. There's no other reason for her to be there. I'm telling you. She knew.'

Bobby and I exchanged a look. Finally, he cleared his throat and turned back to Chloe.

'If there's something here that needs to be investigated, then Elodie and I will investigate it. That's our job.'

Chloe's jaw locked, but I was certain she was about to give in. Then her nostrils flared.

'Well then,' she said, spinning on her heel, 'it looks like I'm taking a career change, because I'm not letting her get away with this.'

And with that, she marched out of the room.

Bobby let out a long sigh and looked up at me.

'Follow her,' Bobby said. 'Make sure she doesn't get into trouble.'

'I'll go,' Dylan replied, jumping into action, only for Bobby to shake his head.

'No, you've got enough to do. Word's out about the paper being a target. I need you to smooth things over with the advertisers. Elodie'll make sure she's okay, won't you? And that she doesn't do something she'll regret.'

'I'll try,' I replied. How I was supposed to stop Chloe from doing anything when I struggled to do the same for myself, I had no idea. Besides, this wasn't a side of Chloe I'd ever seen. I wasn't sure what she was capable of.

I'd known Chloe was a fae from the moment I arrived at The Oracle, but I hadn't known what kind until a few weeks ago. She'd been at her desk on the phone to her fiancé Mick, when her voice raised in a way I'd never heard before. I tried not to listen in, but it wasn't like she was in a private place. Unsurprisingly, Mick had cancelled on her once again, but while that news didn't shock me in the slightest, what happened next did. The moment she'd slammed the phone down, the wastepaper basket at her feet had burst into flames.

That was when I'd learnt the truth. Chloe was a fire fae. Not someone you wanted to mess with. Still, if we were about to confront a sea witch, I wasn't complaining about having a little extra firepower by my side. Besides my vampire skills, of course.

I made it downstairs just as Chloe was hopping onto her bike.

'I don't know where Prue lives,' I said. 'But I guess it'll be quicker if we take the car.'

The fae's jaw remained uncharacteristically locked, and I was momentarily worried about just how many flammable objects there were around us. But given that she'd gone a month without revealing her powers to me, I figured she had them pretty much under control

'Let me guess, Bobby made you follow me? To make sure I didn't get into too much trouble?'

'Well actually... no, I'm an investigative journalist. This is a story that needs investigating.'

She looked at me, then shook her head and let out a sigh.

'I know you're lying, but you're right. It will be faster driving.'

We drove through Ravens Hollow, heading west.

Ravens Hollow might have been the only town on the island, but there were plenty of small pockets of houses, scattered across the hilly terrain. Not to mention the beaches and coves, which was likely where we were headed, given we were looking for a sea witch, after all.

'Do you really think she'd do this?' I asked, as Chloe steered us down a smaller side road. 'Is she capable of that?'

'Prue Parsons is capable of anything,' she said grimly. 'Honestly, that vlog of hers is vile. You wouldn't believe some of the stuff she posted when she first started. Horrible, salacious stuff. Broke up marriages. Accused people of things they hadn't done. She didn't care who she hurt. She just wanted to make a name for herself. And she has, believe me.'

'But has she ever actually... hurt someone?'

Chloe pressed her lips together tightly. 'I'm not sure. But I wouldn't put it past her.'

We continued to drive until the sea came into view beyond the hill's crest.

'How do you know where she lives?' I asked. 'Have you been there before?'

She sniffed. 'Everyone knows where she lives. Claudine put posters up all around town a couple of years ago, after Prue exposed her affair with a tip.'

'Claudine Rosso?' I said. 'The same Claudine Rosso I wrote the red panda article about?'

'That's the one,' Chloe replied. 'It was crazy. She'd brought him onto the island and everything. She would have been arrested, had Nyrah not done several hardy mind-wiping spells. Claudine lost her husband, her lover, and most of the respect of the magical community.

Don't get me wrong, Claudine was clearly in the wrong, letting someone with no para knowledge into this world like that, but Prue's video was cruel. So Claudine wanted payback. She's got one hell of a vindictive streak, that one.'

'She was at the police station yesterday,' I said, thinking of the way she pointed her finger at me, insisting I needed to be punished for all the elk fur that was being dumped on her doorstep. 'She wanted to press charges for the article I wrote, even though she was the one who gave me all the quotes in the first place.'

'She went to the police?'

'Yeah. She was mad.'

Chloe's expression shifted. I could almost see the change in her thoughts, and even though she wasn't an investigative journalist by title, I was pretty sure she could feel exactly where my mind had just gone. If Parsons turned out to be a dead end, then I knew exactly who our next lead was going to be.

TWENTY-SIX

'Wow. Crappy journalism pays really well,' I muttered, parking up outside a large white house perched on the oceanfront. The windows were double-height, and the front of the house looked as though it might disappear directly into the sea, which, given the resident, it probably did.

As I got out, I drew in a lungful of sea air.

I could smell Prue Parsons. That extra-strong hairspray she used to keep her bright red curls in place clung to the air like chemical fog. But there were other, more earthy scents here too. Salt and stone. Something almost... familiar?

'Maybe it's best if I do the talking,' I said to Chloe as I climbed out the car. But she was already marching towards the front door.

I guessed I was backup today.

'Is she in?' Chloe said, pressing her fist against the

door. 'You should be able to smell her hairspray from here. Is she in?'

I briefly considered lying and telling Chloe Prue wasn't in, just to keep her from doing something reckless, but I wanted answers too. So I nodded.

'Yep. She's in,' I said.

'Good,' Chloe replied, before hammering her fist on the door again.

'Prue Parsons, I know you're in there,' she shouted. 'And we know what you've done!' Her voice rang out over the cliffside breeze. 'The police have already been called. The best thing you can do is come out and confess. Maybe we'll even talk them into cutting you a deal.'

She paused and glanced back at me, lowering her voice.

'That sounded right, didn't it? I don't normally get to do this kind of thing. Covering basketball matches doesn't prepare you for this. But I feel like that sounded good?'

'We don't normally do this either,' I said. 'But it sounded great.'

She flashed me a quick grin, raising her fist again, but before it could make contact, the sound of approaching footsteps hit my ears.

'She's coming,' I said quickly. 'She's coming.'

The door swung open, and warm air rushed out, rich with hairspray and something else. Something earthy. Something far more buried.

'Ladies,' Prue said, offering a wide smile that

revealed two rows of perfectly straight white teeth. If I hadn't known better, I'd have thought she was the vampire, not me.

'What a pleasant surprise. Is everything alright?'

'Don't "pleasant surprise" me,' Chloe snapped. 'Why did you do it? We know you're behind what happened to Diego.'

Prue's eyes widened slightly. 'Oh yes, he was the one causing all the disruption yesterday, wasn't he? How is he?'

'Like you care,' I said sharply. 'Now, I want to know what you did. Was it the doughnuts? Did they only affect magical beings, not ordinary humans? Whatever your purpose was, just tell us how to cancel the hex.'

Prue's perfectly plucked eyebrows pinched inward.

'He was hexed?' she said. 'How terrible!'

Despite her aghast expression, her voice didn't rise even a fraction. As if she already knew what had happened while her heartrate remained perfectly steady.

'I know you were there,' I said. 'I know it was you I followed through the woods. Which means one of two things: either you were behind it because you needed a story, and hexing a competitor was the best you could come up with... or whoever did put the hex on him told you to be there. And if that's the case, we need to know. Now.'

Her smile tightened into something much closer to a sneer. She sniffed dismissively at Chloe, then turned her full attention to me.

'Now, I don't know how things work on your side of

the world,' she said smoothly, 'but here, it's very careless
– dangerous, even – to make such unfounded accusa-
tions. You've no evidence I was there. If you had, I'm sure
you'd have knocked down my door before I posted that
rather impressive little video of mine this morning.'

She tilted her chin, unbothered.

'And as for me knowing who did it? I'm afraid I can't
help you. I just happened to be in the right place... at the
right time.'

'Bull,' Chloe said flatly.

'No,' Prue replied, her voice calm and measured.

'I can tell when you're lying,' I said. 'I can hear it in
your pulse. Not to mention, you tighten your grip. You
rub your thumb and forefinger together, too.'

She looked down at her hand, noted the position of
her grip, and quickly loosened it.

'Well then, Miss Evergreen,' she said, arching an
eyebrow. 'Let me tell you this. I do not know how your
friends were hexed. I had nothing to do with it at all.'

'But you do know who did it,' I said.

'You know, you come at me for journalistic integrity,
and here you are, wanting me to divulge my sources. You
trespass on my land, hammer on my door, and threaten
me.'

'I don't remember threatening you,' I said.

'Let's just say the threat was implied,' she replied
coolly. 'Either way, we're done here.'

With that, she turned and slammed the door.

We stood there in silence for a beat or two before
Chloe finally spoke.

'What does that mean?' she asked.

'It means we watch Prue Parsons. Carefully,' I said.

TWENTY-SEVEN

Back at the Oracle, Dylan and Bobby were deep in conversation out in the main office, though they immediately fell silent the moment we stepped inside. Chloe marched straight to her desk and dropped into her seat with a dramatic huff.

Hello. Hello. Elodie. Hello. Chloe.

Pongo pushed his buzzer, welcoming us back into the office. Normally, him using her name button was enough to make Chloe gush all over him, but it was a sign of just how mad she was that she didn't even crack a smile.

'Hey Pongo,' she said flatly. 'That woman is a witch. And I don't mean in the magical sense. I mean, she's a B-I-T-C-H.'

Spelling out a word was the closest that Chloe could get to swearing, and it made me love her just a little bit more.

'How did it go?' Dylan asked, moving across to Chloe, but directing the question at me.

'She knows something, absolutely,' I told him. 'But she's not going to tell us. That's for sure. What about here?' I asked, shifting the topic. 'Found out anything more?'

'Well, word's definitely gotten around to the advertisers that The Oracle is being targeted,' Bobby said grimly. 'They wanna know if they should pull their ads. Couldn't be worse timing,' he groaned.

'Do you think that's deliberate?' I asked. 'I mean, the advertisers pull support, then the big California newspaper sweeps in to "save" us? Feels a little too convenient, doesn't it?'

'Possibly,' he said, though the doubt in his voice lingered. And still, I hadn't mentioned The Guardians to them. Or the whole Claudine Rosso situation. Both were angles that needed to be explored. Though first, I needed a drink. The coffee Whip had got me felt so long ago it was also hard to believe it had only been that morning.

'I think I need a cup of tea,' I said. 'Anyone fancy joining me in the kitchen? I've got a few thoughts I want to discuss with you guys.'

'Sure,' Bobby sighed, his single eye focusing on me intently.

'I could do with something stronger,' Dylan replied. 'And I could also do with some time not on the phone. So count me in for a chat.'

As I switched the kettle on, I turned to the pair of them.

'I've been thinking,' I said, unsure how to start. 'I know we said the paper might be the target, but it could also be personal. And if that's the case, we can't ignore the fact it might be The Guardians. They could be coming for revenge. For me.'

Bobby pressed his lips into a thin line.

'I'm not going to pretend it hadn't crossed my mind,' he said. 'But from everything I've read and heard, it just doesn't feel like their style. Everything they've done so far, it's all been vampire-centric. There's been no mention of any other type of magic. No werewolves or shifters. No other paras. This'd mean they've got someone who could make hexes on their side. Warlocks, witches. Fae even.'

'And you don't think they could have?'

His mouth moved as he physically chewed the question over.

'They might. But I don't know. Part of me thinks they'd want to keep that kind of thing secret. But I could be wrong.'

'What about Claudine Rosso?' I said.

'Claudine Rosso,' Dylan repeated, surprised. 'The red panda shifter? Why would she do that?'

I filled them in on the fur incident, and on what had happened with Prue Parsons and the affair exposé.

'Surely she'd have done one or the other,' Dylan said. 'Either go to the police or hex us. Seems strange she'd do both. It'd immediately make us look in her direction. Maybe a distraction? The way that Theodora and Diego were talking, saying people needed to know, maybe having her tip lover's memory wiped made her want revenge. You know, expose the entire para community.'

'That'd be a damn big revenge. With a damn big punishment to match if she was caught.'

As the kettle boiled, I pulled three mugs down from the cupboard, though before I could grab the tea bags, Diego tapped my arm.

'Remember what I said about wanting something stronger? Look what I found.' He held up a small bottle. 'Mango hooch. Who's up for a shot?'

Mango hooch wasn't exactly the drink I imagined a bunch of journalists sipping at work. Whisky or scotch felt more standard. But I wasn't going to say no right now.

'I'm game.'

'Me too,' Bobby said as he pulled down a couple of glasses, only for Pongo to start pawing at his leg.

'This one's not for you, boy,' Bobby said with a chuckle. 'You can't have this.'

'He's probably after a snack,' I said. 'Given that we're having one.'

Normally, just saying the 'S' word was enough to send Pongo rushing for his buttons and pushing that one repeatedly until we gave in and gave him what he wanted. But it was like he didn't hear. Instead, he continued to scratch at Bobby.

Bobby held out the glass so Dylan could pour. 'Wanna check if Chloe wants one too?' he said, glancing at me.

'Sure,' I turned around, and headed back into the office to ask Chloe if she wanted to join us for a drink, though given how her fiancé was the one who brewed the island's hooch it probably wasn't much of a treat to her.

I was only a step out of the kitchen when my phone started buzzing. When I pulled it out of my pocket, Whip's name was flashing across the screen.

'Hey.'

'Hey,' I said, wishing I didn't feel that little rush of adrenaline at the sound of his voice. 'Everything okay?'

'Not sure. Could be good news. Could be bad.' He paused for a breath before he continued. 'Test results are back. Nyrah and Vincent are pretty sure the hex was ingested. Imbued into a food or liquid and consumed. But Nyrah has fully tested the doughnuts... and there's no sign of anything on them.'

'Meaning?' My stomach twisted, as if I already knew the answer.

'Meaning it was something else in the office. Something else they ate. Is there anything else it could be?'

My gaze shot up to Dylan and Bobby, just about to lift the glasses of mango hooch to their lips. There hadn't been a bottle of hooch in the office yesterday when I'd left. I was sure of it.

'Stop!' I shouted, dropping the phone as I lunged forward and smacked the glasses out of their hands. 'You can't drink that! It's the hooch that did it. The hooch's been hexed!'

TWENTY-EIGHT

Whip and Vincent were there within ten minutes. The three of us had rushed out of the kitchenette and closed the door behind us, as if that would somehow stop the magic effecting us. Fortunately, the men hadn't had a single sip before I'd swiped the glasses out of their hands. Whip had told us explicitly to touch nothing, and as such, the shattered glass remained spread over the floor as we huddled together on the other side of the office awaiting Whip and Vincent's verdict.

Despite his stature and normally calm demeanour, Bobby seemed the most shaken.

'Thanks boy,' he said, crouching to ruffle Pongo's fur. 'You knew, didn't you? You were trying to warn me.'

'Mango hooch,' I murmured. 'It just seems... crazy.'

'But it makes sense that Diego would've had the bigger portion,' Dylan said. 'And Theodora has a thing for the tipple, too.'

The door to the kitchenette opened, and Whip and Vincent stepped out.

'Was I right?' I said, not really directing my question at either of them. 'Was it the hooch?'

'It certainly looks that way,' Whip replied.

'I'll take this straight to Nyrah,' Vincent gestured to the metal box in his hands, which I assumed held the offending items. 'It would also explain why she wasn't able to detect it. Judging by the sheen on that glass bottle, it's leaded. The magic would've stayed hidden within it, even when she was casting her spells.'

'Clever thinking,' Whip exhaled. 'How are you all doing? That was a close call.'

'Not gonna lie, that shook me proper,' Bobby replied, straightening up. 'Good job we've got this one on hand.'

He reached over to Chloe's treat jar and pulled out another snack for Pongo. In the last ten minutes, I was sure he had fed him over half the jar, and any more and Pongo was likely to be sick, but clearly it was what Bobby needed. I'd just have to give Pongo a smaller dinner than normal.

'I've got to head back to the station,' Whip said, looking between me and Bobby as he spoke. 'I'll inform the others as to what's happened, but hopefully now we've found the source, it should make tracking it down a lot quicker.' He offered me a quick look, implying that he was done with speaking to everyone. As subtly as I could, I moved over to the other side of the room so we had a little privacy.

'Thank god I rang you when I did,' he said, taking my

hand so that our fingers interlocked. 'If I hadn't... well, it isn't worth thinking about. Look, I have to go, but I'll call you as soon as I can.'

'I understand, honestly,' I said. 'Go do what you need to do. I'll be fine.'

It was a sign of just how lost in their thoughts people were that even Chloe didn't spot how Whip bent to kiss me on the cheek before he left, though as he disappeared down the stairs, I noticed just how quiet Chloe had gone. She sat silently at her desk, her gaze unfocused.

'Chloe,' I said, walking over. 'Are you okay?'

When her eyes met mine, they were red-rimmed, though I hadn't even noticed she was crying.

'Not really,' she scoffed sadly. 'We all know there's only one place in Ravens Hollow that brews mango hooch. Mick and his brother.'

I glanced at Bobby, just to check to see if he was listening. It felt like the type of discussion we needed to have together. Unlike me, he hadn't moved when Whip and Vincent left and was still feeding Pongo treats, so he was well within hearing range. Still, with a dip of his chin, he implied I was meant to head up this conversation.

I picked my words carefully. 'Chloe, I know this is a horrible thing to ask, but you don't...you don't think they'd be behind this, do you?'

She sniffed, releasing a tear that trickled down her cheek.

'I don't think so. Mick wouldn't hurt a fly. But Larry...' she added, uncertainty tightening her voice.

'It's fine,' I said. 'You don't have to say anything to me. I shouldn't have asked. I'm sure the police will get there soon enough, but maybe it'd be better if Bobby and I spoke to them first. Prepare them.'

Chloe nodded again. 'Thank you,' she said.

'Dylan?' I asked, looking across the other side of her desk, where Dylan was watching on with a box of tissues in his hand, no doubt to give them to Chloe.

'No worries,' he said. 'I'll get Chloe home.'

He moved around and placed a hand on Chloe's shoulder. Her eyes rose to meet his.

'What would I do without you?' she said softly.

'Lucky you're never gonna have to find out,' Dylan replied, his voice so full of love it tugged at my heartstrings. 'Come on, let's get you back.'

After packing up Pongo's buttons, so I could head straight home afterwards if I wanted, Bobby and I left the pair of them and headed downstairs.

'We okay to take the truck?' Bobby said as we pushed opened the door and stepped out into the daylight. 'Not sure I can handle being crammed into that matchbox of yours.'

'I'm not the one you have to ask,' I said, nodding at Pongo, who was already sitting loyally by the Mini.

'It's not going to be long before he's too big to argue with,' Bobby said with a sigh. 'So I might as well make the most of it while he is. Come on, boy. My truck this time, maybe yours next.'

With a disgruntled bark, Pongo trotted over to Bobby's truck.

'So,' I said once we were on the road. 'What do you think about the possibility of Mick and his brother having something to do with this?'

Bobby's eyes remained on the road. He clicked his tongue once against the roof of his mouth.

'You want the answer I'd give if Chloe were in the car, or the truth?'

'The truth, obviously.'

Despite how close Chloe and I had grown, I didn't know Mick at all. Chloe'd tried to arrange for us to meet a few times – dinner by the beach, coconuts at the surf shack, even a working brunch – but every time, something'd come up and he'd had to cancel. Usually last minute.

This was the first time I'd spoken to any of our colleagues directly about her fiancé, and clearly Bobby had a... less-than-favourable impression.

'I dunno what she sees in him,' he said at last. 'And ain't like she couldn't find someone who would treat her a whole lot better.' I was fairly certain that he was talking about Dylan, but I didn't say as much. I didn't say anything. I just let him carry on. 'Mick ain't as bad as his brother,' he sighed a moment later. 'But that don't make him a good egg, neither.'

'So you *do* think he could do something like this? That one of them could?'

'I dunno. They skirt the edges of the law alright, but I'd be surprised if they'd risk upsettin' their business. They've built up an empire, that's for sure. I figure it'd depend on how big a payday they were getting out of it.'

It wasn't exactly comforting.

Despite not having met Mick or Larry yet, I knew where they worked; the garage, or "auto shop" as they called it over here, on the outskirts of town.

A stout man was out front, peering under the bonnet of a car. When he stood up, his clothes were spattered with oil, and he wore his cap backwards. His face was grazed with stubble, the kind worn by someone who couldn't be bothered to shave, rather than someone going for a look.

Considering the effort Chloe always put into her appearance, I couldn't quite imagine her with someone like this. But maybe I was being judgemental. Looks weren't everything. Although, based on the number of times Mick had let Chloe down, and the arguments I'd overheard, I had my doubts about his personality too.

'Is that Mick?' I asked Bobby.

'It is indeed. Don't worry, they're never far apart.'

After cutting the engine, Bobby stepped out of the truck, at which point Pongo jumped out after him and bounded around the front of the vehicle. Clearly, the excess number of treats Bobby had given him had had a definite bonding effect.

'Hey Bobby.' Mick stood up and wiped his oil-slicked hands on the seat of his jeans as he spoke. 'Everything alright with the truck?'

'Truck's running great. Larry checked it over a couple of months ago. I'm actually here for work.'

'Work?' A frown line formed between Mick's brows.

'Yeah, had a bit of an incident at the paper. Where's your brother?'

Mick wiped his hands on his trousers for a second time, though this time, his eyes fell on me, slowly running up and down my body in a way that's pretty vile when any man does it, but even worse when you know that he's engaged to one of your friends.

'I don't believe we've met.'

'No. But we probably should've done, several times,' I said. 'I'm Elodie Evergreen. I work at The Oracle. With Chloe.'

Ignoring my clearly pointed remark, he turned back to Bobby and me.

'What's this about?'

'We'll explain,' Bobby said, moving in towards the building. 'But we need to speak to Larry, too. But you might want to make sure you tell us the truth, because I'm pretty sure the police are on their way.'

TWENTY-NINE

'This is ridiculous!' Larry said, full of the kind of irate outrage only someone who is guilty of something can really manage. Though whether or not he was guilty of the hexing was yet to be determined.

'You run an illegal hooch business,' Bobby replied. 'You don't get to be indignant.'

'We don't poison people. We don't hex them!' Larry snapped.

'Well, I mean, sometimes our proofs are a little stronger than they should be,' Mick added. 'But generally, that's not something people complain about. Makes the nights even more fun, if you get what I mean?'

As he finished talking, he bit down on his bottom lip, looked at me with an oily smirk, and winked. It was all I could do not to gag.

'This isn't a joke,' I said firmly. 'Mick, your concoction was used to put a magical hex on people. If you know anything, anything at all, we need you to tell us.'

'We don't control what people do with our liquor once it leaves here,' he huffed, clearly disappointed that his supposed charms weren't working on me. 'That's up to them. Half the island, if not more, enjoys our hooch.'

'Then I'm going to need a list,' I said.

'A what?'

'A list of everyone you've sold to in, say, the last six months.'

Both Mick and Larry snorted simultaneously, a noise that sounded suspiciously like a pig's grunt.

'You have to be joking,' Larry continued with his outrage. 'There's no way we can do that. Absolutely not.'

'And is that because half your patrons are underage?' Bobby said, folding his arms. 'Because I'm sure the police would love to know that, too.'

'You'd better mind what you're saying here,' Larry snapped. 'That's a serious accusation.'

'As serious as what the people in the hospital are going through right now? Their skin is turning to bark. Did you know that? Bark. Like on a tree. It's taking over their whole body. You know, maybe the best way to stop this happening again is to make sure that no one ever touches your hooch again. I mean, if we put a piece in the paper, declaring that we have no idea how many bottles of contaminated product there are out there, that'd stop orders pretty quick, don't you think Bobby?'

'I think we have a civic duty to let people know what they're putting in their body,' Bobby nodding in agreement. 'We should probably get back to the office now and write that one up, don't you think?'

A frisson of satisfaction rippled through me as the mechanics exchanged a worried look.

'Look,' I continued, softening my tone a little, 'maybe you can't get the names of everybody, but surely there are some you remember. This wasn't just a prank. Someone targeted the paper. If they'd had their way, it would be all of us in those hospital beds, not just two of our colleagues.'

'You mean this could've got Chloe too?' Mick said quietly.

'Yes,' I said holding his gaze. 'She was only safe because she was out of the office. It could've got all of us.'

He nodded solemnly, casting a wary look sideways at Larry. 'I can't give you all the names,' he said. 'I dunno them all. People come and go, but we do have folks we deliver to. I can give you those.'

'It's a start,' I said.

As Mick set off to the office, Larry followed him.

'What are you doing?' he hissed, clearly trying to whisper, though I felt no guilt at all about tuning in. 'Those are our clients! Business confidentiality and all that.'

'That's something you just made up,' Mick replied flatly. 'Besides, these two are right. The police won't have to ask. They'll just take what they want. Unless the reason you don't want me to show them is because you had something to do with it.'

'I didn't!' Larry said quickly.

I tuned into his heartbeat. It had been racing earlier, and this exchange wasn't helping. Still, I could detect no lie in that last sentence. He sounded rattled, not guilty.

'Let's just give them the names,' Mick said with a resigned sigh.

Moments later, the pair returned, holding a thick folder.

'I can't let you take it, obviously. We've got all our orders and deliveries in there. But you can take photos.'

'Thank you,' I said. 'How long does the hooch last exactly? Does it have a shelf life?'

'Never lasts long enough for people to find out,' he replied, that oily smirk back on his lips.

He opened the folder, and I couldn't help but feel a pang of surprise. It was an impressive operation. The first page alone listed deliveries for just half the week, and it was packed. No wonder they barely needed to run the auto shop at all, though I supposed mangoes were seasonal.

I raised my phone and began snapping photos of each page, though my eyes were already scanning the names.

There was a bulk order for Welcoming Woods, where Ines and her pack were based, and another for Wraith Wood, where I knew a couple of packs of werewolves lived, and even one for Weirdoughs, not to mention a couple of other bars in the town. I was surprised to see Nyrah's salon had ordered 3 bottles for the week too. It looked like The Oracle was the only establishment not getting weekly deliveries.

But scattered among the bulk orders were plenty of single or double-bottle deliveries, and some names jumped right out at me.

Claudine Rosso.

Prue Parsons.

Both the women I suspected. The evidence was building.

'You got what you need?' Larry said, cracking his knuckles. 'We do have work to do here.'

I took a last couple of snaps, then looked up at him and offered my sweetest smile.

'All done. We'll be in touch if we need anything else.'

From the way he grunted, he was absolutely delighted with the prospect.

'I KNEW Prue had something to do with it,' I said as we drove back towards the paper. 'We need to get Whip to question her properly.'

My verdict was still out on Mick. I didn't like the guy much, but it had been the thought of Chloe – not us – that finally spurred him into standing up to his brother and getting us those names. And for that, I was at least a little grateful. I was pretty sure I heard him pick up the phone to call her as we left too. Maybe he'd be a better boyfriend from now on.

Still, I couldn't take my eyes off the photo on my phone. Or more specifically Prue Parson's name and how she'd had four bottles of mango hooch delivered to her house in Pepper's Bay only a week ago.

'Admit it,' I said to Bobby. 'You know she's guilty.'

He let out a long sigh.

'Come on Elodie, you know how this works. She's not going to give up her source. She'd rather go to prison.'

'But would she?' I challenged. 'It's not like her vlog's an actual paper. I reckon if you squeeze her hard enough, she'd crack.'

'I wouldn't be so sure,' Bobby replied.

I was surprised by how much credit he was giving Prue, but though I'd defer to Bobby's knowledge when it came to most of the island's residents, this was different. I'd had Prue's number pegged the moment I found out she was the one who'd shared the photos of me in the lion onesie.

'She didn't even deny it was her in the woods. Of course it was her – she had that video!'

'Maybe we should just run an article on her,' I suggested. 'I don't know. Try to spook her a bit.'

'Got anything particular in mind?'

'No,' I admitted. 'But we have to do something, don't we?'

In the back of the truck Pongo let out a soft whine, nudging the back of the passenger seat.

I twisted around the best I could to look at him.

'I know, boy, I know. You've not had many big walks this week, have you? I'll take you for one today, okay? Is that—' I didn't get to finish.

The air whooshed out of my lungs as Bobby slammed

on the brakes. My body jerked forward in the seat, the seatbelt digging so sharply into my chest that pain seared up my shoulder.

'What happened!'

I turned to look at Bobby, while simultaneously rubbing the back of my neck. His expression was tight. Focused.

'Sorry about that,' he said, though he didn't so much as turn to face me. His eye was fixed straight ahead. 'You know what you said about your number one suspect? I think you might be wrong about that one.'

I followed his gaze to where he was looking, just a short way in front of the truck. We were on bridge road, just beyond the turn that led to Pepper's Bay. There she was, walking towards us with the all-too-familiar vacant stare of someone hexed, muttering to herself, holding her bark-like palms out ahead of her.

Prue Parsons had been hexed.

THIRTY

'It's all part of a plan,' I said to Whip when he turned up ten minutes later.

I hadn't bothered trying to accost Prue or even see if she could hear. Instead, I'd got out of the car, and with Pongo at my side, followed her from a safe distance to see where she was going. She was muttering the same nonsense Diego and Theodora had been. Something about people knowing. And she was walking the exact same path; down the main road that led off the island.

She had almost reached the edge of Wraith Woods when Whip pulled up and clamped the cuffs on her.

Like with Diego, her whole body went limp. A sign of how much had been given to her? I wasn't sure, but if that was the case, then it was definitely a fair amount.

But then, I wouldn't have put it past her to down an entire bottle just for effect.

'I know you don't get on with Prue,' he said as he

lifted her into the back of the police car. 'Honestly, not many people do – but we still have to treat her like any other victim.'

'She's not,' I replied firmly. 'She took that video of Diego yesterday. She was the one I chased into the forest. She as good as admitted it. And she's had a delivery this week of mango hooch. Which, might I remind you, was the conduit for the hex? She is behind this. I'm sure of it.'

Whip's gaze narrowed. 'You really don't let go when you get your teeth into something, do you?'

'No, I don't,' I said, trying to ignore the way his smile was twitching at the corner of his lips. 'And this is not the time to look cute and handsome and make me want to kiss you, because I'm not going to do it.'

'I wasn't making you want anything.' His smirk took full form. 'But it's interesting to know that you want to kiss me. I'll keep that in mind.'

I was not supposed to be flirting. I was supposed to be making sure Prue Parsons was locked up and couldn't hurt anyone else – although, at that precise moment, she was slumped in the back of the patrol car, entirely unconscious.

I was about to push my case a little further when Whip's phone buzzed in his pocket.

'I need to get this,' he said. 'It's Vincent. Hopefully he's got something. Maybe Nyrah's figured out how to lift the hex.'

As Whip stepped away, I sidled back over to Bobby and Pongo.

'It didn't sound like your boyfriend was too keen on arresting our unconscious sea witch,' Bobby said.

'Firstly, he's not my boyfriend,' I muttered – though that phrase was already looping unhelpfully in my head. 'And apparently she has to be treated like any other victim.'

'And now he's on the phone to Vincent,' Bobby added. 'Be good to know what they were saying.'

His eyes twinkled. I knew exactly what he meant. He wanted me to listen in to the private conversation of the Chief Inspector. A man who had a distinct possibility of becoming my boyfriend. Would I have hesitated a week ago? Not in the slightest. But now? Now it felt like crossing a line.

A jolt ran through me. After everything with Andy, I'd promised myself that I would never change who I was for the sake of a man. And regardless of how good-looking, or magical, not to mention what an incredible kisser Whip might be, the same still applied. If old Elodie had the opportunity to grab a major scoop, she wouldn't have given that up, just because the guy it might upset was super hot.

With my mind made up, I turned my back on Whip.

'Make sure it looks like we're having a conversation,' I muttered to my boss.

'Sorry, you want me to do what?' Bobby frowned.

'That's great, just keep talking like that,' I replied, then shifting my focus, blocked out everything Bobby was saying and tuned in to Whip.

'But if you know what's caused it, you can make an antidote, right?' Whip was saying. 'Lift the hex.'

'I've already started work on it,' Vincent's voice came through clearly. I was definitely getting better at controlling my vamp senses if I could hear what people were saying on the other end of a phone. It was cool. Scary, but cool. 'But that's not the issue.'

'Then what is?'

The extent of my new powers stunned me even further when I could have sworn I heard Vincent gulp. And the sound didn't make me feel good.

'I need this to be off the record, Whip,' he said after a pause. 'This could have serious implications for me. I can't have it come back on me. Not with everything I do for the town.'

'Okay. It's off the record. Just tell me. What's the issue?'

Vincent paused before continuing.

'I've not managed to isolate the magic that's been used to create the spell, but I have been able to identify the ingredients. One of them is silver mugwort root.'

'Am I meant to know what that is?' Whip replied. So apparently the immortal I was sort of dating didn't know everything. It was a surprising relief to find out.

'It's a plant,' Vincent said. 'One that's very difficult to grow. So much so that there's only one place in Ravens Hollow that I know of that can cultivate it.'

'And where's that?'

'My garden,' he replied. 'Mine and Nyrah's. Behind

the shop. And I've just checked. Our plants have been harvested, recently. And whoever did it took a lot.'

Silence perforated the conversation, though I could hear the increase in Whip's pulse.

'What are you telling me?' Whip said. 'Explicitly?'

'Whoever's behind this had access to our garden. And the only people who have that, are Nyrah's employees. One of them is behind this. And they took enough silver mugwort root to hex the whole damn island.'

CHAPTER
THIRTY-ONE

By the time Whip was off the phone, I'd already relayed the news to Bobby.

'One of Nyrah's employees!' he'd blurted out.

'Shh!' I hissed, shooting him a glare. The last thing I wanted was for Whip to know I'd not only listened in, but disseminated the news to my boss without a second thought. Whip was on the phone again, though. While I didn't listen in, I assumed he was passing on the news to Alex and Raquel at the station.

'Do you know any of them?' I said to Bobby. 'Any of the people who work for her?'

He let out a thoughtful hum. 'June'd be the one to ask. She goes there now and then. Likes to get a deep pore steam facial thing done. Whatever the hell that is.'

'Facial.' The word flung me back to first thing that morning. 'Bobby, one of Nyrah's employees came to my house today. She wanted to see if I was okay. What if she was checking, because she was the one who'd done it?'

'Who was it?' Bobby asked, his single visible eyebrow arching.

'Amira,' I said. 'She's a fae.'

'I know the one. Ears go straight out.'

'That's her. Could she be behind it?'

This time, his eyebrow rose as he pondered the thought. 'Never had any trouble before. She's not from Ravens Hollow originally. Must have been here, oh, twenty years, though. Think June's had her over for drinks a couple of times. I'll ask her.'

Before I could say anymore, Bobby shot me a look, and I turned around to find Whip striding towards us.

'Good news?' I said, trying to look casual; like I hadn't just eavesdropped on my maybe-boyfriend.

'Vincent's worked out what's in the hex. Some of the ingredients, at least. It's a step towards an antidote.'

'Amazing,' Bobby said, smiling broadly. Too broadly, actually. Maybe it was because I knew what we'd been discussing, but the expression looked unnaturally cheery. Like he was trying to hide something. Bobby was great under pressure. I'd seen that at the paper several times already. But great at lying? I was starting to think that wasn't one of his fortes.

'We should get back,' I said, keen to get my boss out of there before he dumped me in it. 'See what we've got to do, article-wise and all that.'

'Right.' Whip's eyes remained locked on mine.

'And you probably need to get back too,' I said. 'Of

course you do. I mean, you have to get Prue to the hospital. And you need to tell the others whatever it was that Vincent just told you on the phone. If he told you anything, that was. And if you haven't already told them.'

Crap. So much for thinking that Bobby was going to be the one to give me away. I was well aware that if I didn't shut up soon, I was going out myself. We needed to get out of there ASAP. I turned to leave, but before I could take a single step, Whip reached out and caught my hand.

Pongo growled.

'It's fine boy,' I said, grateful for how my dog had my back, even if it was completely unnecessary. Not that Whip paid him any attention. His gaze was fixed solely on me.

'Elodie...'His voice was that deep drawl that caused me to shiver in all sorts of inappropriate places. 'You wouldn't be thinking of doing anything silly now, would you?'

'Silly? Why would you think that?'

'I don't know.' His lips twitched ever so slightly. 'But if I had to bet on whether or not you'd *want* to listen in on my conversations, I'd say yes. But you wouldn't do it, right? Because that would be illegal. And you wouldn't break the law like that, would you? Not when you're so new to the magical community.'

'Me? Break the law?' A strained laugh cracked in my throat. 'No, no. Absolutely not. Of course not.'

'Not to mention it would be a violation of trust. Our trust.'

'Right. Of course.'

His eyes narrowed on me. I kept my smile fixed, but I could feel it faltering, and it didn't help that my throat had suddenly grown inexplicably dry. And no amount of swallowing would clear it.

Whip lowered his voice further as he took another step towards me. I could feel the heat radiating from his body.

'Elodie, I'm serious about this. I'm crazy about you. You know I am. But I've got a job to do. And if being with you starts to compromise my integrity as Chief Inspector, then we've got a problem. You understand that, right?'

I didn't want to understand. I really didn't. But I did. This wasn't like Andy, moulding me into something I didn't want to be. This was different. This was figuring out how to be with someone I liked without losing myself.

'You trust me, right?' he said, his voice now a near whisper.

'Yes.' The words left my lips at a similar volume. Almost too quiet to hear.

'And you trust that I'll do my job?'

'Yes.'

'Okay, and I trust that you can do yours without crossing any boundaries we won't be able to come back from. Is that fair?'

I dipped my chin in a nod, but before I could reply, Whip planted a kiss on the top of my head, turned, and walked away.

THIRTY-TWO

Annoyed wasn't half of what I was feeling. I was frustrated, angry, confused. I was irritated that Whip was right, of course, that I had overstepped a mark both personally and professionally, but I was also pissed that he thought a kiss – albeit an incredibly sweet one – would be enough to silence me. If that was why he had done it, of course. He may have just wanted to kiss me goodbye the way he had at my house this morning. But we weren't at my house. We were at work.

Bobby had slipped off at some point during my conversation with Whip and got back into his truck. As I let Pongo into the back and climbed into the passenger seat, my boss offered me a sympathetic smile.

'I seemed to catch a bit of that,' he said.

'The bit where he rightly accused me of breaking the law, or the end bit.'

'Both,' Bobby admitted. 'And while I've not been in

exactly the same position as you before, I am aware of what it was like when Raquel first got the job at the station. Finding that balance, to not affect her integrity or how people viewed her as a police officer with what I did, was really hard.'

'So how did you get past it?' I asked. 'What did you do?'

Bobby let out a sigh that was far deeper and more heartfelt than I would've liked.

'We definitely had a few low days,' he said. 'But in the end, we set boundaries. Sometimes it's difficult. She feels like I'm overstepping, and maybe I am. Maybe I feel like she'd be different if it wasn't her dad trying to get these stories. But I love my job, and I love my daughter even more. So I had to make it work.'

As we drove back into town, Bobby's words continued to play on my mind. He had been right in saying it was different, though. Raquel was his daughter. Flesh and blood. They were bound for life

Whip and I weren't bound together. We were...I didn't even know what Whip and I were. Was it something I was willing to give up a career I absolutely adored for?

I didn't think so. But then, I didn't think I'd ever find myself daydreaming about a single dimple, desperate for him to return. I didn't think a single kiss would ever be enough to make my knees go weak. So really, I didn't have a clue. That was what it came down to.

Back at the station, Dylan was sitting with Chloe, his

hands resting on top of hers. The second we came in, they jumped up.

'You spoke to him, didn't you?' she said, ready to start with her normal barrage of questions. Still, it was better than when she wasn't really talking at all. 'You spoke to Mick, right? I just got off the phone with him. He seemed worried about me. What did he say? I'm so angry. I should've come with you, but then I'd been too furious. Did he tell you anything that helped? He said he did, but I don't know if he was telling the truth.'

'Mick was helpful,' I said. 'Certainly more helpful than Larry.'

She let out a long sigh, visibly relieved by this news. 'Well, that doesn't surprise me. Larry is like all the worst bits of Mick without any of the good bits. So, did you find out anything?'

'Actually, we found out quite a few things,' I said.

I held up my phone. 'They let us take a photo of all the people they delivered mango hooch to in the last couple of weeks. And guess whose name was on it?'

Chloe's eyes widened. 'Prue Parsons?'

'Bang on. But also Claudine Rosso. But here's a spanner in the works. Actually, a couple of spanners.'

'I don't think they need to know the other bit of information that we had,' Bobby said, staring at me pointedly. He was talking about what I'd overheard, but there was another factor I wanted to address first. 'Bear in mind, it still could be a ploy.'

'What could be a ploy?' Dylan asked.

Damn it. I was a journalist. I had to look at all the

evidence objectively. But with someone like Prue, that was incredibly hard.

'We saw Prue on our way back into town,' I said.

'You did?' Chloe asked. 'What was she doing?'

'She was walking. Walking down Bridge Road, towards the north of the island.'

Chloe's face paled.

'You mean she was going to meet someone for a story?'

'No, she wasn't,' Bobby said. 'What Elodie means to say is that Prue Parsons has been hexed too.'

'What?' Chloe said. 'But how?'

'Like I said, I think it's a ploy.' I wasn't going to let this go. Prue knew to be there to record Diego. It wasn't a coincidence. 'But there's something else we need to think about, too.'

I was well aware that Bobby was right, and there needed to be boundaries in place between Whip and me, but at the same time, I couldn't forget what I had heard. And it seemed silly not to share it with them.

'Vincent called Whip while he was there sorting out Prue, and he's identified some of the ingredients that were added to the mango hooch to make the hex.'

'That's good news, isn't it?' Chloe said, hope causing her voice to rise.

'Does that mean they can make a cure?' Dylan asked. 'That Diego and Theodora will be okay?'

'Fingers crossed,' I said. 'I didn't get that far. But there was one thing Vincent did mention, and that was that the ingredients he found could only have come from one place: the garden at the salon. The one that Nyrah and her staff use.'

I gave the other two a moment to catch up to what we were saying.

'You're saying that one of the people who works at the salon is behind it?' Chloe asked. 'They did this to Theodora and Diego? But who? Why?'

'Whip's looking into it now,' I said. 'With Vincent. But I thought maybe we could have a dig around too. See if there's anybody who might have a reason to attack the paper. Also, I had a visit this morning from one of the employees and that feels like a bit too much of a coincidence.'

'Which employee?' Chloe asked.

'Amira. Do you know her? She's a fae.'

I felt rather presumptive adding that last bit. Just because Chloe was a fae, it didn't mean she knew all the other fae folk that lived on the island. It wasn't like I knew a single other vampire in town. I was sure there had to be plenty, given that Weirdoughs catered for our particular dietary requirement, but so far my path just hadn't crossed with any of theirs.

'Amira?' Chloe shook her head. 'No, there's no chance. She won't do magic. Of any sort. She used to babysit us as kids, when she first arrived. All the adults who used to babysit us would do really fun tricks, you know, like grow flowers or turn our drinks into ice, but she'd do none of it. She used to make us colour, or play music, or bake, and stuff like that instead. Tip stuff.'

'But she can do magic?' I said. 'She could if she wanted to?'

'I'm not sure,' Chloe shrugged. 'I heard some of the adults say they thought she'd been stripped or born muted, but she never integrated herself. She had a flat by the seafront in the centre of town, and after a couple of years, she stopped coming over. I can ring my cousin Elise, though,' she added. 'She's a hairdresser, and she's got a shop about four doors down from Nyrah's place. She's constantly there and knows everybody on a first name basis and knows all the gossip, too. If there are any grudges or anything untoward going on with any of those people, Elise will know about it.'

'Amazing,' I said. 'Can you get her to come in?'

'Sure. I'll ring her now.'

As she moved over to the side of the room with her phone, Pongo nudged my knee.

I took his buttons out of my bag and placed them on the ground.

Immediately, he hit one of the buttons.

Tired. Tired.

'Me too, boy,' I said with a sigh. 'Me too.'

THIRTY-THREE

'Guess who I've just got off the phone with?' Bobby strolled back into the main office half an hour or so after we'd returned. The rest of the time, he'd been squirrelled away in his own office, and I'd noticed that he'd shut the door a little over ten minutes beforehand to take a call. I'd made a concerted effort not to listen in, although, given how he'd been the one who encouraged me to eavesdrop on Whip and Vincent's call, he could hardly have blamed me if I had.

'Was it Vincent?' Chloe said, immediately on her feet. 'Has he lifted the hex? Are they okay? Can we see them?'

Bobby's face fell at her reaction. 'No, it wasn't Vincent. Sorry,' he said, clearly regretting the way he'd started the conversation. 'It was the Cali Chronicle.'

Now that made me sit up and take notice.

'What were they ringing for?' I said. 'Have they heard what happened? Has it reached the mainland? What did you say?'

I was aware of just how like Chloe I sounded, but I had to give it to her, there was something incredibly cathartic about getting all your questions out in one long stream, even if Bobby looked somewhat confused by my sudden outburst.

'Yup, they'd heard. And wanted to assure me they'd nothing to do with it.'

'The fact that they needed to clarify that should be a sign that they were seriously overstepping the mark with how much they harassed you,' Dylan said.

'Maybe,' Bobby agreed. 'But they've said they understand we have a lot to deal with, so I won't be hearing from them for a couple of months.'

'A couple of months. How generous,' I muttered, only to realise how negative I sounded. Their looming presence had probably been a weight on Bobby's mind for some weeks now, and he had some respite from that, at least. 'Sounds like we need a bit of a treat to celebrate,' I said, keen to make up for my momentary slip into negativity. 'I'm going to pop to Weirdoughs and grab some things. Now, who wants what?'

DID I HAVE A CAFFEINE PROBLEM? Quite possibly. Was that going to stop me getting my second Weirdoughs drink of the day? No. Absolutely not. It helped me think. Then again, it could have been the blood that did that. I didn't know. But either way, I wanted to get out of the office as much as I wanted my drink.

Even though I was at home at the Oracle, I didn't have my own sources. My own people. I had to wait for the others to come through for me. Like Chloe with her cousin, and that came with frustrations I wasn't used to dealing with. Hopefully, the drink would help. And it meant that Pongo got a bit more of a walk, which I knew he wanted, too.

'Hey, Omar,' I said, grateful that I finally knew the name of the gentleman who served me daily.

'Afternoon,' he grunted, making no attempt to reciprocate the knowledge of names. But I guessed he dealt with a lot more people on a daily basis than I did.

'Omar, what's the biggest dose of blood you can put in one of these things and, you know, make it not taste like blood?' I asked

He let out a dry chuckle. 'Amazes me how many bloodsuckers don't even like the taste of the stuff. But then, I guess once you do, you don't bother comin' to me no more. I could do a triple-shot mocha with a shot of caramel syrup in it. That covers up all the red stuff.'

'Fantastic,' I said. 'Only... could you make me two?'

'Rough day?'

'Something like that,' I said. 'And I need a couple of other things too.' I proceeded to list off the items the others had asked for, and couldn't help but notice how much shorter it was without Diego's requests. When he was finally well again, I'd get him one of everything they had here, and I was pretty sure he'd be able to eat it in one sitting.

'Just be a couple of minutes. Gotta finish loadin' up a box o' pastries for takeaway.'

'Those? They look like flowers,' I said, gesturing towards the box at his side.

'Petal pastries,' he clarified. 'Ninety percent flowers, ten percent honey. So not pastries at all, but the sprites love them. Anyway, why don't you take a seat? I'll be with you in a moment.'

While he disappeared towards the coffee machine, I glanced around me. Weirdoughs was generally packed in both the seating area and the bakery takeout side, and today was no different. There were barely any seats free, but I spotted an empty chair at a table with someone I actually knew. Hoping she'd be as amenable as her sister was whenever we stopped for a chat, I moved over to her.

'Hey, Sophia. You alright if I sit down with you? Just for a minute.'

The amber eyes of the werewolf looked close to bulging from her head.

'You want to sit with *me?*' she said.

'If it's okay. Just for a minute,' I replied. 'I'm just waiting for a drink, that's all.'

'Oh.'

Sophia was a spitting image of her sister. From her eye colour, to her earthy nature and even the slight formaldehyde aroma that came from her aunt's unusual gifts. But while Ines and I were not what you'd call friends, conversation had always flowed fairly easily between us, and I'd expected it to be similar with Sophia. I couldn't have been more wrong. Instead, I was faced with a wall of stony silence. Silence I was struck with a desperate urge to fill.

'I spoke to Ines yesterday about the council meetings,' I said, clutching at the first straw I could think of. 'We were talking about how good it is that they're finally looking into the hunting grounds.'

'Sophia, your order's ready!' Across at the bakery, Omar lifted a large box and waved.

'Well, that's me.' Relief washed visibly over Sophia as she stood up and pushed her chair back. 'I'd like to say the conversation was pleasant, but... you know.'

As the door to the cafe swung closed behind her, I glanced down at Pongo, who offered me a slight whine.

'Wow,' I said, rolling my eyes as I spoke. 'Remind me not to get on the wrong side of her.'

THIRTY-FOUR

Back at the office, Chloe was sitting with a woman I didn't recognise, though the moment they saw me, they were both on their feet.

She was dressed in a ruby-red corset top, her hair crimped in an almost 80s style. I had to admit, I loved this side of Ravens Hollow. Yes, it was a small-town community, and as Sophia had shown me, gossip and grudges could easily fester and spread. But there was also an unspoken rule that people wouldn't be judged for being themselves. If you wanted to wear a corset top, go for it. If you wanted to knit jumpers out of your red panda's moulted fur...

No, scrap that. If what Claudine Rosso had said was true, then she had been judged quite harshly for that. But, for the most part, it was an incredibly accepting place. I suspected that came with being a power-heavy community.

'Elodie, this is my cousin Elise,' Chloe told me. 'She

had the afternoon off, so I asked her to come here. I was about to ring you, but obviously you're here.'

'Amazing. Thank you,' I said, before lifting up the bag of pastries. 'I was just going to put these in the kitchenette first.'

Chloe pouted.

'Maybe we should just put them on one of the tables out here,' she said. 'You know... rather than going in there.'

It was a good point. Vincent had assured us the place was safe to use, given that he'd cleaned up all of the spilled hooch and taken the rest of the bottle with him.

'I'll take them,' Chloe said. 'Then you can have a chat.'

She took the box, at the same time, calling Pongo over to her. There was no chance we were going to have a treat without him having one, too.

'Thank you for coming down, Elise,' I said, pulling out a chair and gesturing for her to take a seat. 'Did Chloe tell you why we asked you to come?'

Elise nodded. 'Yes. It's about the stuff going on at the salon today, right?'

'Yes.'

'Well, if you want the latest from Nails and Naughtiness, Walden's been sacked.'

'Walden?' I wasn't familiar with the name, and if I was honest, I was almost certain Amira was going to come up as number one suspect. It still felt wrong, the way she had appeared at my house. But right now, I was collecting facts, not acting on my hunches.

'Rumour is that Nyrah gave them all a truth serum the moment she'd heard the root had been taken. It's in their contracts that she can do that apparently. And let's be honest, no one can resist one of Nyrah's potions. I've heard she's so powerful she can put a glamour on you to make you look entirely different. I was thinking I might ask her if she could make me a couple of inches taller, you know? Maybe a full foot.'

'But about Walden,' I said, trying to redirect her back to the reason we'd called her in.

'Right.' A pink tinge coloured her cheeks. 'Well, according to some people, he's going to be arrested. But I can't go on record as saying anything. I've already told Chloe that. But I don't mind talking to you, if it'll help with the hex thing. I'm a hairdresser, see. People tell me things. Lots of things. But if they think I'm going to spread news to a journalist every time I hear something juicy, my business is done for.'

'There's no way we'd do that. Absolutely not,' I replied, lifting my hands to stress my point further. 'We just want to know what happened to Diego and Theodora, and why. The why's the bit that really matters right now, because if these people have something against us, something against the paper, then we need to stop them before anyone else gets hurt. We need to protect ourselves.'

'I get that. I do.' She steepled her index fingers together and pressed them against her top lip while taking a deep inhale in through her nose. 'Honest to God, I can't think of any reason Walden would've taken umbrage with Theodora or Diego. Or any of you at the paper, for that matter. Prue Parsons, maybe–Chloe told me about her. Not sure if she was meant to, but I won't tell anyone. Anyway, Prue did a horrible piece about Walden when he was a trainee; said she'd rather get her nails done by a troll in a cave than let him touch her again. But that was... oh gosh, twelve years ago now.'

'And Walden's been working for Nyrah all this time?' I asked.

She nodded. 'Absolutely. I mean, he's her go-to person. I think he actually wants to start up his own business now. Not sure if he'd do it in Ravens Hollow or not, but that's been his aim for the last few years.'

'Starting up his own business...'

'What are you thinking, Elodie?' I jumped at the sound of Chloe's voice behind me. I hadn't realised she was there.

'Well, starting a new business is expensive, and I can't imagine salons are any different. Actually, I expect they're even more expensive than a lot of places. He'd likely need to set up a garden for ingredients like the one Nyrah's got out the back of hers. That's a whole other cost, along with basic furnishings, rent, not to mention staff.'

'You mean you think he sold the hex ingredient for money?'

I nodded. 'It would make sense. That's why most people do things. Particularly if there's no revenge motive. Thank you, Elise,' I said stretching out my hand to hers. Given what she'd already told me, I didn't think there was any need to keep her any longer. 'I really appreciate it.'

'You're absolutely welcome,' she said. 'And... do you need to book in an appointment?'

'An appointment?' I asked, confused.

'For your hair,' she said.

'Oh. Right, yes.' I tugged at the end of my strands, aware of how brittle and dry they felt. It wasn't that I didn't like to do my hair or take care of myself, it was just that it always slipped down the priority list. But then, maybe if Whip and I were going to go on an actual date, it wouldn't hurt to make a bit more of an effort.

Of course, I still wasn't sure how this relationship of ours was going to progress and there was no point starting anything if moving forward was going to be an absolute impossibility.

'I'll give you a ring,' I said. 'Thank you again for your time.'

'No problem,' she said.

As Chloe set off to see her cousin out, I sat down at my computer. I had just opened my emails when a shadow loomed over me.

'Can I help?'

I was surprised to find Dylan hanging on my shoulder. Chloe and I would often wander over to each other's desks for a chat, but Dylan tended to spend most of his time either on the phone, answering emails, or out at business meetings. I couldn't remember a single time when he'd come over and stood next to me like this.

'I know what I do isn't much use to you with this,' he

said. 'But if there's anything I can do to help, make full use of any of my contacts, or anything to help get to the bottom of this, you'll let me know, won't you?'

I smiled, a pang of gratitude tightening in my chest. Every day, I loved this paper more and more. The camaraderie, the friendships; it was something special. And I had worked with my best friend for years.

'Thank you, Dylan. I appreciate that, I really do. And if I think of anything, I'll absolutely let you know.'

'Sure. Right.'

With that, he turned around and headed back to his desk. I finally opened the first email in my inbox. It had no title, yet I clicked on it.

The moment I did, my blood ran cold.

THIRTY-FIVE

I picked up my laptop and walked straight into Bobby's office, closed the door behind me, and placed my computer on his desk. Pongo managed to sneak in, but I didn't need the others to hear this.

'I need you to read this,' I said.

We know what you are and where you are. Do you know the answer to both those things too?

That was all the message said.

'It's from The Guardians, isn't it?' I tried to control the tremble in my voice. I should've known that when you kill a vampire who's been taking money from typicals to change them, it wasn't going to end well. And in the back of my mind, I'd been waiting for this moment. 'It's them, letting me know they're out there. That they can get me.'

Bobby drew in a long breath. 'It does look like that,' he said.

'Do you think it was them that did the hexing too?' I asked.

'Honestly, I don't know. Maybe if it'd just been at this paper, I would have said yes. But Prue Parsons? How does she fit into their plan?'

'Assuming she didn't do it herself to throw us off her scent?' I said.

His single eyebrow quirked at me. 'Yes, assuming she's a victim.'

I pondered the question momentarily, but it really didn't take that long to come up with a viable explanation for Prue's sudden hexing.

'What if she needed to be kept silent?' I said. 'She was involved. I know that. So maybe someone told her to be near Wraith Woods to get that film of Diego. But then she started getting a little too close for comfort.'

'It's certainly a possibility,' Bobby admitted. 'Though you know what you need to do with this now, right? You need to take this to Whip.'

A long sigh bellowed my lungs. 'I know. It's just... I'd rather not do it today, you know? After the conversation we had earlier, you know, I feel like things might be a bit awkward with us.'

'Didn't look that awkward when he left,' he said.

I recalled the kiss Whip had given me. The tenderness. I doubted he would have done that if he was really mad at me. But still, going to the station meant Alex was going to be there too, and if he found out about this email, he might suggest we stop digging into The Guardians, the way I was certain Whip was going to.

'Whip has access to all sorts of information,' Bobby interrupted my musing. 'We like to think we're the first port of call for everything, but Whip has access to things we have to wait for. Like, Floyd will always answer to him. He could make him set up notifications for anyone unusual coming onto the island, for instance. Not to mention get Nyrah to place wards at your house.'

'It's not like I'm never going to leave the house,' I said. 'And she can hardly ward me against a vampire, can she?'

'I know. But still. It's worth thinking about, isn't it?'

'Yes. Yes, I guess it is.' I let out a long sigh, and Bobby gave a nod.

'No time like the present,' he said.

I let out a groan. Of course, he was right.

'Come on, boy,' I said, looking down at Pongo. 'How do you fancy seeing Josephina?'

AFTER PACKING UP MY COMPUTER, I decided to walk to the police station rather than drive and not only because Pongo had spent a fair amount of time cooped up or waiting around. I was looking for any reason to delay my talk with Whip. I was a vampire now. I was meant to be stronger, invincible compared to when I was a human. And sure, in a physical strength way, I was phenomenal. But this kind of thing? Being taunted by email? My colleagues being attacked? Just made me feel weak and hopeless, and I hated it.

Still, as I stepped out to a familiar figure waving at me from across the parking lot, I realised there were people I wanted to talk to even less than Whip.

'Elodie! How lovely to see you.'

'Claudine?' The last time we'd spoken, she'd been ready to turn me into the police for the outcome of the article I'd written. And now she was smiling at me. Widely. There was also a cluster of people behind her, mostly middle-aged women, but a couple of men and some younger people, too.

'Is everything all right?' I asked.

'Oh, everything is wonderful. Wonderful,' she gushed. 'This here is my little knitting circle.

'Elodie, such a funny thing happened,' she continued. 'You know those bags of fur that were left outside my door?'

'The ones that were ruining your life?' I said. 'The reason you went to the police?'

'Hahaha, yes,' she let out a strained laugh. 'Well, I didn't realise it, but they were gifts. Gifts from lots of these lovely people here who were hoping I'd be able to do with them what I did for me. So anyway, obviously I don't have enough time. Not with all the commissions I've got going on, so I'm teaching everybody how to knit with their own fur. Isn't that wonderful?'

'Wonderful,' I repeated, with more than a slight edge to my voice.

'Well, thank you ever so much for the article. It really was wonderful.'

'Right,' I said.

'And if you want to do a follow-up on the knitting circle at any point—'

'I'll let you know,' I said, already turning around and offering her a wave.

Yes, Claudine Rosso was not someone I was going to work with again in a hurry.

The next person I recognised was stepping out of the police station just as I arrived. June, Raquel's mum and Bobby's wife.

'Elodie,' the woman said, wrapping her arms around me in a motherly hug. 'How are you? Is everything okay?'

'Bobby rang me this morning. I heard about what happened with the hooch. I was just dropping some food in for Raquel and the others. You know how hard they work. They'd never leave the station if I didn't make them.'

I'd had dinner at their house a couple of times since I moved, and though I loved the idea of being brought lunch to my desk, I couldn't help but wonder how much of these deliveries to the station actually got eaten. June was a smart woman with many talents. Cooking was not one of them.

'I'm sure they're very grateful,' I said.

'We all do what we can, don't we? You know, I used to bring them to the paper, but Bobby told me to stop. It wasn't that they didn't like them, just apparently Diego would polish everything off before anybody else got a chance.'

She smiled, then seemed to realise what she'd said, and her expression suddenly fell.

'I shouldn't I... I didn't think...'

'It's fine, June.' I placed my hand on her shoulder. 'We've all said exactly the same about Diego at some point. I just hope they manage to find this cure for him and Theodora soon.'

'Yes, absolutely. Is that why you're here? To see if there's been any progress?'

June was a siren, and whether the ward I had from Nyrah worked against *all* sirens, I wasn't sure. But then, I doubted June would use her power like that, and thankfully, I had no issues avoiding telling her the truth.

'Yes, that's why I'm here,' I said.

'Well, I won't keep you,' she said. 'And take care of yourself, Elodie.'

'I'm trying to,' I said, gripping my laptop a little closer.

The moment we stepped into the station, Pongo started barking in delight at the sight of Josephina. It was like it had been weeks since he'd seen her, and the way her face lit up was a clear indication that she felt the same.

'Hello, boy,' she said, patting her knees and calling him towards her, even though she couldn't see much of him. 'Are you going to catch me? I bet you can't! I bet you can't!'

'Hi, Josephina,' I said, feeling the need to acknowledge that I too was there, and not just my dog. 'Are you all right if I leave him here with you for a minute? I need to go and talk to Whip.'

'Yes, yes. Go, go,' she said, waving me away.

Josephina'd said before that the police station used to have dogs. That's why we got Pongo's bed and everything from here. And I think she really missed it.

I made a mental note to mention it to Whip. Perhaps the idea of getting her a station dog was worth following up. It wasn't like she wouldn't keep it entertained, even if she couldn't take it for walks. Though discussing it with him would have to wait. We both had other things to deal with first.

THIRTY-SIX

As I stepped into the main part of the station, Raquel looked up from her desk.

Though the police officer had her dad's impressive height, her smile was identical to her mum's. Also, unlike her father, she sported two, deep blue eyes, not that I'd ever seen under his eyepatch to confirm my suspicions about what type of para he was. 'Hey Elodie.'

'Hey, I just saw your mum outside. Said she'd dropped off some food for you.'

Raquel grimaced. 'Alex has just popped out back to get rid of it. If it was him you were looking for?'

'Actually, I wanted to talk to Whip.'

'Oh, right.'

I wasn't sure if it was my imagination, but I could have sworn there was a flicker in her eyes.

'Can I go straight in, or is he busy?'

The blinds to his office were down, though I could already hear that there was no one in there with him, nor was he talking to anyone on the phone, but it hardly seemed polite to say as much.

'He's pretty stressed, but I'm sure he'll be happy to see you.'

'Thanks,' I said, flashing her a smile I didn't feel.

There was no chance that what I was going to tell Whip would make him any less stressed, and I wondered whether I should leave my issues until later. But I needed to talk to him about them at some point. Just like we needed to discuss setting boundaries, the way Bobby had suggested. Whether Whip's place of work was the right location to do it was debatable, but there was no time like the present. And better to get it all out in one go.

That was what I was hoping, anyway.

With nerves bubbling through me, I knocked on the door.

'Come in.' His deep voice resonated through the walls as I twisted the handle and stepped inside. 'Elodie?' He hurriedly stood up from behind his desk. 'Is everything okay? Is this about Diego and Theodora?'

'No, it's not.' I stepped into the office and closed the door behind me. 'It's not about them, I mean. Actually, I'm not sure. It could be. But it's not really alright either. At least I don't think so. It's about me, though.'

Whip tilted his head. 'I'm not sure I understand.'

I could hardly blame him. For someone who worked with words, it was embarrassing how unintelligible I could be sometimes. With a deep, steadying breath, I pulled my laptop out of my bag and tried again.

'I received an email earlier. Bobby thought I should show it to you.'

Whip's lips pursed, drawing in his cheeks and accentuating those obscenely sharp cheekbones of his.

'What did it say?'

In an almost identical manner to the way I had done with Bobby, I placed my laptop down on his desk and gave him a moment to read through the email. Not that there was much to read.

'From theguardians@paramail.com,' he said after a moment. 'If it's not them, then it's certainly someone who wants to make you think it is.'

'I know. That was my thought too, actually. Maybe it's just somebody trying to scare me, but I've no idea who would want to do that.' Other than Prue Parsons, I didn't dislike anybody on the island.

'We probably need to ward your house,' Whip said. 'I'll get Nyrah onto it as soon as I can. Right now, she's still struggling to work out how to lift this hex. But I'll send an alert to Floyd. Get him to check for unknown vampires coming in. I need to go off island this evening anyway, so I'll talk to him then.'

'You're going off island again? Already?' I didn't mean to sound so disappointed, but he'd only been back twenty-four hours. Though with the amount that had happened in that time, it seemed hard to believe.

'Just for a couple of hours. Nothing big. I was still hoping I'd be able to see you when I get back. If it's not too late. And after reading that email I'd feel better staying at yours too, if that's okay. Just on the sofa again. Until we can get the ward in place.'

Whip was doing exactly what Bobby had said, he would do, notifying Floyd and enlisting Nyrah's help, but the sleeping over... Yes, I wanted him to stay the night, but not because he thought I needed protection.

'It's not like I'm powerless,' I said, feeling an overwhelming need to point this out to the immortal siren. 'I'm a vampire too. And I've got Pongo. I'm sure I'll be fine.'

A loud bark echoed from the corridor, as if he knew we were talking about him.

'I know you're not powerless,' Whip said. 'But I want to be there for you. I hate to think of you being in danger.'

'I get that, I do.' I realised we were slipping into the other part of the conversation I'd wanted to have with him, without explicitly saying so. 'But sometimes my job leads to me being in precarious situations. Just like yours does. I don't think I need to remind you that I was the reason you got Macoy Belkin.'

'I'm well aware,' Whip said with a near groan. 'And your passion for your job is one of the reasons I admire you so much. But at the same time, I can't jeopardise my job. And you listening in on my conversations? It'll do that. People'll think you're only sticking close to me so you can get your next scoop.'

I couldn't believe anyone who saw Whip would think that for even a second. Would they think I was with him purely for his looks? Absolutely. That would make way more sense. But it didn't seem like an appropriate time to say such a thing.

'We need to be able to separate the professional and personal,' I said instead. 'If we actually want to make something work, then we need to put boundaries in place.' I felt a thrill of satisfaction at getting Bobby's buzz word in, but it was a relief to see that Whip was nodding in agreement.

'I agree. Absolutely. And in case I haven't already made it obvious enough, I want to make something work. So how do we do that?'

The way his lips twitched with a smile caused a flutter of excitement in my belly, but it was quickly extinguished. Cops and journalists had notoriously tempestuous relationships. The thought of building that into something romantic was incredibly difficult, to say the least.

'So,' I said, 'the listening in on your conversations is a no, right?'

'Yes, Elodie,' Whip said, with a hint of exasperation. 'Definitely a no.'

'I was just clarifying,' I said, lifting my hand in defence. 'I get that. And I'm genuinely sorry about this morning. So, I guess that would be rule number one. No listening in on police conversations. Or any of your conversations.'

His lips cracked into a smile. 'They're really not that exciting, if I'm honest. But maybe that's a good place to start. And when it comes to the whole vampire powers thing, how about no racing ahead of me to crime scenes so that you get there before the police?'

'What? No way,' I said.

'Why not?' His brow crinkled. 'I'm not saying don't use your vampire powers, just don't put yourself in danger. Or do anything to the crime scene.'

'If I had a motorbike or a faster car, I could easily get there before you. If a source rang me, I would get there before you. There are dozens of possible reasons that would mean I'd arrive at a crime scene first. That's an absolute no from me,' I said.

He let out a soft laugh. 'Okay, so you're not going to budge on that. But can we at least say that you are not going to approach any situations in which you find yourself in danger?'

'Do you remember how I got turned?' I said, arching my eyebrows, only to step forward and place my hands on top of his, before staring directly up into his eyes.

'Look, how about this? I behave mostly as I would've done as a human reporter. I don't listen in on police conversations, but I will still use my vampire senses if I think it's going to help. This is a para community, after all. You're just going to have to trust my judgement.'

He chewed my proposition over.

'I do trust your judgement,' he started. 'But if you do hear anything. Or smell anything, or see anything that could be important to a case or even remotely criminal, I need you to notify me, okay? I can't be worried that you're hiding things from the police just because you want the scoop.'

'Well, I'll still get the scoop, right?'

It was his time to arch an eyebrow.

'You're the only paper on the island. Of course you're going to get the scoop,' he said.

For a moment I considered mentioning Prue Parsons, but I was fairly certain Whip was as repulsed by her methods of journalism as I was. Besides, there was another matter I still needed to bring up.

'Also, no kissing me when we're working. Even if it is just a peck on the forehead.'

I held his gaze fixedly and watched as a flush of embarrassment colour his cheeks.

'That may have been a lapse. But you are incredibly kissable.' He smirked. It was the first time since I stepped into the office that his smile had been wide enough to cause that dimple and I could already feel my knees turning weak at the sight. With his eyes still locked on mine, he took another step closer. 'And by "working," does that include when we're in an office, with the blinds closed and no one is able to see us?'

'What did I say about boundaries?' I said, fully aware of the adrenaline that was rushing through my body.

'I wholeheartedly agree to them all,' he growled, his voice a low rumble that reverberated all the way down my spine. 'I was just checking if they started now, or once you leave this room...'

THIRTY-SEVEN

Whatever game Pongo and Josephina had been playing, Pongo was worn out, sitting in the corner panting, with his big pink tongue lolling out of his mouth. Sometimes I wondered if I needed to take him for walks, when fifteen minutes here seemed to tire him out. Then again, walking him had helped me see more of Ravens Hollow, and there was still the rest of the island to explore. Although I'd need to wait until he was a bit bigger before he could manage that.

'Elodie,' Alex stood up from his desk the moment I stepped out of Whip's office. 'Amazing. You're here. I wanted to talk to you.'

'Hey,' I said. 'How've you been? Hectic I'm guessing.'

He rolled his eyes before flashing a grin. 'That's one way of putting it. You okay?'

'As okay as I can be, I guess. I'll feel better when Nyrah works out how to lift this hex.'

'Yeah,' Alex's grin dropped. 'I heard she's finding it tough. Apparently, it's not any type of magic that she's used to.'

'Really? What type of magic is it?' I'd not even thought of there being different types of magic. That fact that magic existed had been a big enough hurdle.

'I'm sure she'll work it out soon,' Alex said, hurriedly, obviously worried he'd let too much slip. 'But I actually wanted to talk to you about something else.'

'Something to do with The Guardians?' The thought of the email on my laptop burned within me, but there was no need to worry Alex about it, too. Especially when I didn't know what he'd found out.

He nodded. 'I was going to say something yesterday, but obviously with everything going on, it didn't seem like the right time. But as you're here—' he lowered his voice, 'I was looking through some old notes and found something that might be of use. But we can talk about it later, if you want.'

'No, I'd like to know now.' I said, unable to rein my eagerness in. 'As long as that's okay with you.'

'Sure.' He dragged a chair over for me to sit on before taking his own seat. 'I said there were no known people from The Guardians, or with unknown sires, turning up in Ravens Hollow in our recent records, right?'

'That's what you said.'

'But I was only looking back to when we updated our computer system, which was around eighteen years ago.'

'You haven't updated your computer system for eighteen years?' I asked, raising an eyebrow.

'Well, it's had minor updates, but it's been running the same software since then. Doesn't matter. Anyway, I went back to the old records. And as it turns out, there was one vampire with an unknown sire who turned up in Ravens Hollow about twenty years ago.'

'Twenty years ago?' I let out a long breath. The Guardians had been working that long? Twenty years ago, I was nine years old. It was the worst year of my life. The year my mum decided she was done being a parent and wife.

'And it might be a complete long shot, but I thought it might be worth going to see them.'

'They're still on the island?' A flutter of excitement gripped me. Even if they weren't turned by a Guardian, there was another vampire with an unregistered sire here. I wasn't the only one.

'They've got an apartment overlooking the main stretch of beach in town,' Alex continued. 'I haven't contacted them, though. I don't know when would be a good time to go. We're pretty manic here. I'm guessing you're the same.'

'Absolutely. But I'd rather see them sooner rather than later,' I said, thinking about the email.

Alex's eyes met mine. 'Has something happened?'

'No, no. I just... you know. Like to stay on top of stuff.'

His gaze lingered on me, like he could tell I was lying, and for a second I assumed he was going to press me some more, but instead, he simply offered a swift nod.

'Well, she's been here for twenty years. I doubt she's going anywhere. But we can go whenever you want.'

'Okay. Great. Thank you, Alex. I'm not sure today would be the best. But maybe tomorrow?'

'Sure thing.'

It was hard to ignore the spark of hope which had ignited in me, but I tried not to let it catch. After all, twenty years. What were the chances that it was someone turned by a Guardian? It had to be pretty slim, didn't it?

'Thank you, Alex,' I said as I stood up before looking over to Pongo. 'Come on, boy, we should get going.'

My dog's big hazel eyes were sagging, and it was clear he wanted nothing more than to go to sleep.

'Elodie?'

I turned around to find Whip standing in his office doorway. 'Do you have another minute before you go?' he asked. 'I've got something that might be of interest to you.'

Given how ten minutes ago I had been in his office with the blinds down and his lips on mine, I assumed his object of interest would not be something he'd share with the others in the station. That was until he started walking towards me.

'What is it?' I frowned.

'Well, I guessed you were going to go digging into what you learned from Vincent earlier in the day, so I thought I'd save you two the time and tell you what happened with Walden.'

'Walden?' It took me a moment. 'The one who works for Nyrah?'

With all the chaos from the email, I'd almost forgotten. 'Sure,' I said, only to carry on before he had a chance to speak. 'It was money, right? That was why Walden gave them the plant. Money to buy his own salon. But did he tell you who it was?'

A light chuckle cracked from Whip's throat. 'Of course, you've already been digging. I should have realised that.' He let out a slight sigh before he carried on. 'Yes, it was for money, but no, he didn't say who it was from. He didn't know. He just got a letter requesting it with an initial chunk of cash. It said he had to respond by leaving a cactus in the window if he agreed. And more cash would come. Which it did.'

'And that's the letter?' I asked, noting the envelope in his hand.

He handed me the page.

I couldn't help but grin as I opened it up. 'Look at us. Police and press working together?'

I glanced down at the letter, reading it aloud.

'I'll pay twenty times this if you get me silver mugwort root. As much as possible.' That was all it said. The words had been printed, meaning there was no handwriting to go on, while the paper appeared to be standard white printer paper. Something most people had at home.

'Straight to the point,' he said. 'I wondered if you could pick anything up from it. Smells or anything.'

It was my turn to smirk as I raised an eyebrow.

'Chief Inspector Whip, are you enlisting the help of a journalist now?'

'Just asking a question, that's all,' he said.

I lifted the paper to my nose and drew in a long inhale, only to cough and choke the moment I did.

'Elodie?' Whip's hand was on my back, slapping it repeatedly as I coughed again as I struggled to regain my breath. 'It's just... a lot to take in.'

I was struck by dozens of scents. The person definitely lived in Ravens Hollow, and the fact that this had been in the salon was no surprise either, as intense aromas of acetone and varnish caught at the back of my throat. That much was clear. I could smell salt, maybe sea air. I could also smell a strong waft of coffee. Though I wasn't sure if that came from the paper or myself. But there were other smells, too. Dozens of them, tightly mingled. Earthliness. Woods. Leather and something more chemical...

'Well?' Whip asked.

'I'm not sure,' I said truthfully.

Taking another, slower sniff. Yes. There was definitely something earthy in it. And mango hooch.

I handed it back to him.

'Something's familiar. But I'm not sure why. There's nothing I can identify that you don't know. The salon. The hooch. But there is something else. I promise, if I realise what it is, I'll tell you straight away.'

'Okay.'

For a second, we stared at each other. And I felt like he was going to kiss me goodbye. I absolutely wanted him to. But I took a step back.

'Ring you later?' he said with a flash of a smile.

'Sounds good,' I said, before calling Pongo over to me and walking out the door, determined to identify that mystery scent. It was the key to finding our criminal. I was sure of it.

THIRTY-EIGHT

B ack at the paper, Bobby was still there, waiting for me.

'You alright?' he asked. 'What did Whip say?'

'About?' I blinked. 'Oh, about the email?'

He nodded.

'Yeah, sorry,' I said, shaking my head. 'It's been a lot today. Well, he's doing what you said, working with Floyd and the team on the bridge, and getting Nyrah to do some warding. But Alex said she'd had difficulty working out what magic was used to create the hex, and that's her priority right now.'

The look of worry remained fixed on Bobby's lips. I was pretty sure I was about to get a lecture on keeping myself safe, and so offered a swift change of topic before I could.

'Whip also showed me the letter Walden was given.

The one offering him money to get the plant for someone.'

'He did?' Bobby's eye widened. 'And?'

'And it smells. Lots of different smells. I'm sure I recognise one of them, but I can't figure out why. It's a scent from somewhere that I've been in Ravens Hollow. And it's not like I've been *everywhere*, but still.'

'Maybe you need to look at a map of the island. See if anything sparks a memory.'

'You have a map?' I asked. The entire island was cloaked in magic, meaning that I'd not even known it was an island when I'd first arrived. The only map I'd got of the town was one Bobby had drawn me on my first night here to show me how to get from my house to work – though he had also labelled Weirdoughs on it for obvious reasons. Every other location I had learned by walking Pongo, or driving in my Mini and the idea of seeing it all laid out flat so I could actually understand the geography had me more than a little excited. And not just to help with the case.

'It's a little old, but the main places are on there.' He opened a drawer in his desk and pulled out a hefty folded piece of paper.

'Amazing. Thank you,' I said, desperate to unfold it then and there, while well aware that it would take ten times longer to fold it back together.

'Want some help? Don't mind going through it with you if you want?'

He looked at me expectantly, but I shook my head.

'That's alright. I thought I'd look at it at home, if that's okay. It's been a pretty long workday.'

That was putting it mildly. From waking up to the knowledge that Pongo probably wasn't hexed, to discovering mango hooch had been the hex's source, to questioning Mick and Larry, seeing Prue walking hexed down the road, and then the email and heart-to-heart with Whip. Yup, it had been an incredibly long day, and I was ready to take off my bra and sit on a comfy sofa.

'You sure?' Bobby asked. 'Maybe being on your own after that email from The Guardians isn't such a good idea. Why don't you come back to our place? June'd love to have you for dinner.'

I tried to keep my expression neutral as I thought of Alex and Raquel disposing of June's cooking out back, so she wouldn't know. But beyond the questionable food, I wouldn't be great company. My mind was too occupied with other things to hold a proper conversation. I needed to look at this map.

'I'll be fine. Honestly. Promise.' I picked up my phone and turned it towards him. 'You're my top contact if I need help. And I've got the police station on speed dial.'

Of course, Whip was going to be off the island for most of the evening, but I didn't need to say that part out loud. Now that I'd seen Alex in his shifter form, I was fairly certain he could tear anyone to pieces without a second thought. And as I'd already said to Whip, it wasn't like I was incapable of looking after myself. I was a vampire, after all.

'Alright. Just take care of yourself,' Bobby said.

On the drive home, Pongo sat curled in my lap. It wasn't very convenient. Classic minis really don't have much room, and I had to push the seat all the way back, and hold him as close to me as possible. But it wouldn't be long until he was too big to do this at all, and I wanted to make the most of it.

'I can't believe that a day ago I was worried you'd been hexed,' I said to him. 'How does so much happen here? So much for a quiet life, right?'

I'd thought life in London was busy, but there, even the most hectic days had been broken up with long stretches of downtime. Waiting on the Tube. Sitting in traffic. Queueing for coffee. Wasting hours in meetings. Here? There was hardly any of that. Sure, Bobby held a weekly meeting. And there were the queues at Weirdoughs. But otherwise, I just seemed to be going from one event to the next.

When I got home, I fed Pongo, placed his buttons on the floor in the living room, then spread the map of the island across the coffee table. Bobby hadn't been joking when he'd said it was a 'bit old.' Ravens Hollow was about a quarter of the size it was now, if not smaller, and there were only a couple of buildings in Pepper's Bay. Almost everything else was forest. The two northern woods were still separate, but what I knew as Welcoming Wood and Folorning Forest were joined with just a single track through them. There were also plenty of places I'd barely heard mentioned, like Calypso Cove and Banshee Bay, though the latter wasn't somewhere I planned visiting any time soon. My previous story had taken me to Pepper's Bay, as had this one, but that wasn't where the scent came from. I was sure of it. So where had it?

Closing my eyes, I tried to remember the exact nuances of the aroma. It was the chemical one that didn't fit in. A chemical I had smelt before. But not varnish. Something different. A flash of memory stirred within me, of animals posed in eclectic, supposedly humorous, manners.

My eyes pinged open. I knew where it had come from. I knew who had sent the letter.

CHAPTER
THIRTY-NINE

It was hard to ignore the fact that, on my raciest story in Ravens Hollow only six weeks ago, Ines Ortega had been my first suspect for the murder of Wren Belkin. And here I was, now, weeks later, ready to tell her that I knew she was behind the hexes that had happened to my work colleagues and friends. I knew why Ines had done what she had done. Things were moving too slowly for her in terms of the council's protective orders and the changes to the hunting laws for packs around different parts of the island, and she had wanted that changed. But I had been trying to help her. I had been ringing the mayor's office twice weekly since we put her and her sister's petition to the council, trying to get answers. I had kept Ines filled in on all of this. For crying out loud, she had even told me two days ago at Weirdoughs how grateful she was for all of my support. And she'd probably gone straight from there to give Diego the hexed drink. So much for me believing one of my vampire superpowers was spotting liars. She had fooled me hook, line and sinker.

'Come on, Pongo,' I said, standing up and folding the map in half. 'We've got a werewolf to talk to.'

I rang Whip, although when I heard the rumble of tyres in the background, I suspected he was already off island.

'Hey,' Whip said. 'I've just spoken to Floyd about monitoring vampires coming in. I'm not gonna lie. It's probably going to make us a few enemies. Some people are funny about giving away their sires and things, but still... it'll be done.'

'Thank you. I appreciate that,' I said.

I paused. He was out of Ravens Hollow, yet I knew he would turn around and come straight back if I asked him. But did I need him? It wasn't a full moon and whoever had done the hexes it couldn't have been Ines herself. She was a werewolf and as far as I was aware, they couldn't even do magic. Then again, there was a lot I wasn't aware of.

'Is there anything else?' Whip asked. 'You okay? Did you work out what the smell on the envelope was?'

I bit down on my lip. We had promised we would share things. That I would let him know if I found anything to help with a case. And this was my chance to prove to him that I was capable of doing that.

'I think so. It's formaldehyde,' I said. 'Used in taxidermy. I think Ines has done this. You know... to raise awareness of the woods. I can't be sure, but I reckon if we'd let the people who'd been hexed keep walking, they'd have ended up in one of the woods that has been over hunted because of the restriction. Force people to see how bad it is for the creatures out there.'

The rumbling of the road continued down the line as he let out a long breath.

'I'll send the others over there. You don't need to go near that place, you understand, Elodie?'

My muscles clenched.

'Whip, it's six days until the full moon. There's not much of a risk. And I'm a vampire. And I'm halfway there. We need to get her now, before she knows we're onto her.'

'She won't know we're onto her, unless you tell her,' Whip said, his reasoning annoyingly logical. 'Are you listening to me?'

'I am. Yes. Yes, of course.'

But it wasn't that simple. I had promised I'd help Ines and clearly I'd not done enough. If I had, she wouldn't have needed to resort to these measures. I needed to talk to her. Find out if there was any way we could approach this that would lessen how hard the police came down on her. Not to mention avoid undoing any positive work we'd already done for the cause.

'You're going to go anyway, aren't you?' Whip said. 'Shit. I'm turning the car around now.'

'You don't have to do that.'

'Yes, I do. I'm ringing Alex. He's got some cuffs, okay?'

'I'll be fine, Whip. I promise. Just meet me there when you can.'

'You are infuriating, you know that?'

'Isn't that the reason you like me?' I replied.

He growled.

'Maybe I should make Nyrah weaken the ward on you next time, just so you'll do what I say some of the time.'

'Absolutely no chance,' I said. 'Race you there.'

I turned off the highway onto the road that led to Welcoming Woods, then continued onwards towards the small hamlet in the middle of the forest where Ines and the rest of the pack lived.

'Ines!' I called out, well aware that with her werewolf hearing, she would be able to hear me. 'Ines, I need to talk to you. I know what you're doing.' I parked up and sprang out of the car, leaving it opened so Pongo could follow me. When I reached the front door, I hammered my fist against it, so hard that wood splintered beneath my knuckles. Crap. That wasn't something I'd expected.

'Ines!' I yelled again, only for the door to swing open.

'Elodie?' she said. She was dressed in jeans and a black vest top, her hair tied back in a messy bun. And there behind her the taxidermy animals. Which now included a mouse riding a raccoon. It may have taken me a little while to figure it out, but I had been spot on with the aroma. 'Is everything okay? I was just upstairs. I heard you calling all the way down the road. What is it? What's happened?'

'I know, Ines,' I said. 'I know, and Whip knows. And you're not going to get away with it. The police will be here any second now.'

'What?' she said, her brow crumpling in confusion.

'What are you talking about?' I had to give it to her, she was a good liar, but I had evidence, and evidence trumped a poker face any time.

'The hexes. You're the one who hexed the hooch. Or at least, you paid someone else to do it. What were you hoping, that by sending people to the forest and seeing how bad it was, it would hurry up the mayor's decision?'

'What? What do the forests have to do with the people being hexed? I thought they were walking down the road?'

Again, her pupils remained exactly the same size as she looked at me, and I listened to her heartbeat. It was steady, although fast. Of course, it wasn't beyond the realms of possibility that an angry vampire knocking on her door would make anyone's pulse race, but still.

'Let me guess. You messaged Prue so that she could be there to record Diego and place it on her blog, but then she put the pieces together, and you had to hex her, too.'

'Sorry, Elodie,' she said, her soft demeanour gone. 'What exactly is it you're accusing me of here? Hexing the paper? Prue Parsons?' I glanced to the corner of the room, where a crate of small glass bottles was sitting with yellow liquid inside. Half the bottles were missing. Mango hooch. As if I needed any more evidence that she was behind it.

'We were working with the council, Ines. That's what you said you would do. And I know it was going slower than you wanted it to, but I thought you would have come to me about it instead.'

'I'm sorry,' Ines said, crossing her arms over her chest. 'Let me get this straight. You're here accusing me of hexing people in this community because the council wouldn't pass my laws quick enough?'

'The letter you gave to Walden,' I said. 'The one promising him money for silver mugwort. I saw it. Whip showed it to me. It smelt of formaldehydes. There's only one place on the island that I've smelt.'

Her jaw dropped. 'Formaldehyde. That's what you're basing this off? Because you smelt formaldehyde. You realise that the funeral home uses it, as do the Peridot wolves, who tan their own leather, not to mention my aunt, who actually makes us these monstrosities. You've come banging on my door, accusing me of a pretty heinous action.' Her jaw locked. 'I'm sorry, Elodie, I get that you're doing your job, but you're barking up the wrong tree, and I'm going to ask you to leave now. That's the only time you're going to hear me ask nicely.'

I noticed two things immediately. The first was that Pongo was just a few feet behind me, trying to look fierce, but really, he was just a brown pompom with legs. The second thing was that several of the surrounding houses had now had their doors open. There was Rumi Hawkins, who lived next door, and his father, along with another dozen people, some of whom I recognised from around town, some of whom I'd never seen before, but all were watching on.

'Whatever you think I've done, you are wrong,' Ines said.

I drew in a long breath, mostly to steady myself, only for a creak to sound from upstairs.

'Who else is here with you, Ines?' I said, practically spitting my words.

'Elodie, I'm warning you—'

'Who else!' I growled.

It had been a long time since I'd lost control of my emotions so much that my fangs flicked out, but here they were. I had to give Ines her due, she didn't move. Then again, maybe that was because she had half her pack starting to circle her house. But did they really think they could take me? Werewolves were only strong when it was a full moon. They didn't stand a chance. Worst-case scenario, I would scoop Pongo up and race out of there, and he'd just have to deal with the head rush.

'There's no one here,' Ines said. 'Just me and Sophia. Now I'm done.'

'Sophia,' I said. My mind flickered to earlier in the day. To sitting with Sophia in Weirdoughs's as I waited for my drinks, and she awaited her parcel of petal pastries. But why would a werewolf eat something like that? They hunted for meat, didn't they? And even if one was a vegetarian, that amount was enough to feed... to feed a forest full of sprites.

I shifted my gaze past Ines to the stairs where Sophia was standing at the top with her arms folded across her chest. As her eyes met mine, a smirk lifted her lips.

'Right conclusion,' she snarled. 'Wrong sister.'

S ophia stared at her sister and while her pulse was steady and strong, Ines's hammered so loud I could hear it. Just like I could hear the tremble in her lungs.

This wasn't a bluff, I realised. Sophia was behind the hexing.

'Sophia,' Ines said slowly. 'Please tell me you're joking. Please tell me you didn't do something this stupid.'

'What's stupid is kowtowing to the Council constantly,' Sophia snapped. 'You still believe they'll actually do something for this island? It doesn't matter how much evidence you show them, Ines. When are you going to realise they don't respond to that? They respond to action. That's what we need to be doing. We need to be acting. Making them see.'

'By hexing innocent people?' A pang of guilt struck at

the way I'd blamed Ines. It was clear from her outright shock that she'd had no idea.

'We need to get the word out.' Sophia remained at the top of the stairs, looking down at us as she spoke. 'Last full moon, it all fell into place. We needed people to see that we're not going to just bow down to this. And the hexing is just the start of it.'

'Oh my God. Do you have any idea what you've done?' Ines gasped before her voice had dropped to a low tremble. 'How did you make those potions, Sophia?'

Sophia ran her tongue across her lips, her eyes darting towards me.

'It doesn't matter how I did it. The truth will be out there. About how much they're damaging the environment. About the power the creatures they're harming have.'

'And we'll be ostracised even more than we already have been,' Ines replied, her voice rising. 'Do you have any idea what kind of risk you've put the pack in? I need to call Dad.'

Ines's father was the alpha of the pack, though I'd never met the man. I wasn't even sure he lived on the island half the time. As her pulse continued to rocket, I looked at Sophia.

'How did you do it?' I said quietly. 'What were the ingredients? How did you make the potions? The hexes?'

Her eyes met mine.

'Tree sprites,' she said. 'The ones that live in Wraith Wood, near the scrying circle. The ones whose homes the

Council insists they're trying to protect but do nothing to help. They were the ones who taught me how to hex the hooch. Amongst other things.'

'You made them? You made the potions and spells yourself?' Alarm flashed across Ines's face. Not just alarm, but fear, too. Sophia just shrugged like it was nothing.

'That's why Nyrah couldn't work out how to lift it,' I said. 'Because it's not any kind of magic she's used to.'

'It sounds likely,' Ines said. Her phone hung in her hand as she looked at me. 'I'm sorry for going off at you. I had no idea. I'll help you get a cure. One hundred percent. Sophia is coming with me to the station now to turn herself in and do everything she can to fix this.'

'Like hell I am,' Sophia growled, her eyes flashing. 'Oh no. I may have admitted what's happening, but there's no way I'm turning myself in. That would make it look like I didn't stand by my values. Like I thought I was wrong. And I don't. I wasn't wrong. It was the right thing to do.'

'Hurting innocent people is never the right thing to do, Sophia,' Ines replied, voice firm.

'But that's what they're doing. All. The. Time. All the sprites, the nymphs, the sylphs. And more too, I bet. They're losing their lives because the balance is disrupted. And they can't just move forests. That's not the way it works.'

I could feel Sophia's fury.

'I am your beta,' Ines said, calm and collected. Far

more measured than I thought anyone could be in a situation like this. 'I am your beta. And you need to obey me. You will turn yourself in.'

Fear shuddered through me. I'd seen this before. Seen what happened when a wolf tried to go against the hierarchy. If a wolf went against their pack's hierarchy, they'd be cast out, exiled. Forced to live alone, away from everything and everyone they'd ever known. I'd been the one to blame at the time, asking questions of a young wolf without realising what I was doing. But Ines and Sophia? They knew exactly what would happen if the younger sister disobeyed.

'Don't fight me on this,' Ines said. 'Don't fight me.'

I stood frozen, no idea what to do next.

'Don't make me fight you for this.'

Ines let out a sound that was close to a scoff. 'You can't take me. You know you can't. I've beaten you in every fight.'

'You're right,' Sophia said. Her voice changed. Sharpened. 'But the thing is, that hex wasn't the only thing the tree sprites taught me to make. It turns out that silver mugwort root has more than one use. And one of them is incredibly helpful to werewolves.'

Ines glanced at me, as if I'd know the answer, but I was as lost as she was.

'What did they teach you to make, Sophia?' I said quietly. 'What is it?'

Rather than replying, Sophia pulled a small vial from her pocket and popped the cork.

'Please. Please don't,' Ines was begging. The certainty

in her voice transformed into fear. 'Whatever that is, you don't need to take it. We can work this out. Talk it out.'

'Talk?!' Sophia's laugh was nasal and bitter. 'That's all you want to do, isn't it? Talk through our problems. Hope they go away. But you've forgotten how Dad became Alpha, and it wasn't by asking nicely. He took that position. With power.'

'Sophia, people will get hurt.'

Ines motioned out of the house to where other members of the pack were gathered, listening in.

'I wouldn't be so sure,' Sophia smirked. 'Let's see how good you are at fighting when you're stuck in your human form. And I've got real power flowing through me. Let's see how long you maintain your beta title that way.'

Then, without another word, she tipped the vial back and drank the potion.

A cold wind swept in from nowhere. She coughed and spluttered, bending double with her weight propped on her knees. She stumbled forwards, rolling down the steps. Her face twisted in pain, a squeal ripping from her throat.

Instinctively, I stepped towards her to help, but Ines threw her arm out, blocking me.

'No. She brought this on herself. You need to get out of here.'

'What's happening?' I asked, but I didn't need the answer. Because I could see it.

Sophia's posture had already begun to change. Her spine elongated, fingers stretched, her body shifted downward. Her long hair grew down her back, on the back of her hands. And her face... her face was barely human any more.

Now I knew what the potion did. It forced a werewolf into their wolf form without the need for a full moon. Ines was in trouble.

CHAPTER
FORTY-ONE

'Elodie you need to move. Get out of here, now.'

Ines's voice was unwavering, but I didn't move. I was transfixed. Unable to draw my eyes away from the sight in front of me.

It wasn't even dark outside, but I was staring at a werewolf. A fully changed, long snout, and foaming mouth werewolf. I assumed seeing Alex transform into his lion form would have been enough to eliminate my surprise at such a thing, but when I had stared at Alex in his animal shape, there had still been some semblance of him. The same kind of peace he carried as a human remained. There was none of that in Sophia. Admittedly, her eyes were still their original colour – the amber of all the amber wolves – only filled with fury, while the way she bared her fangs was entirely animalistic.

'You can't take her like this,' I said to Ines.

'I'm going to have to,' Ines replied, without so much as a glance in my direction. 'It's my duty as beta. I have to fight her. Don't worry, I'll be okay. Go get yourself and Pongo out of here.'

Pongo. Panic surged through me as I looked down at my feet where Pongo had been only a moment before, but the space was empty. 'Pongo!' The slightest whimper caught in my ears and relief broke through as I spotted him, cowering behind the sofa. Sophia took a slow pad towards us.

'Get him and go now,' Ines said.

It didn't matter that I wanted to stay and help her. This was a wolf thing. Yet, as I turned to leave, a new, tighter knot took hold inside me. 'Ines...I don't think Sophia's the only one who took the potion.'

The gasp that left Ines's lips sounded more like a stifled sob, yet she remained exactly where she was, not even turning to look at me as she refused to take her eyes off Sophia. A split second of distraction was all it would take for her to lose everything.

'How many?' she asked.

'Three, I think,' I said. That was as many as I could see, bent double, hunched over the way Sophia had been only minutes before. Others were backing away from them, confused.

'I have to deal with Sophia first,' she said. 'Can you stop them from getting to us?'

'I think so?' I tried to sound confident, but it was difficult. 'Sure, I mean, I'm a vampire. I can take on three werewolves, right?' The question was more to myself than anything else. I glanced at Pongo. 'Stay,' I said, locking my eyes on Pongo. 'You hear me? Don't move. I'll come back for you, okay?'

With that, I stepped outside.

I'd been wrong.

There were four turning now, and a couple more people had vials in their hands. That had to be my first action; stop more from changing, so I could deal with the ones that had already turned. In the distance, I could hear the rumble of an engine. A car coming up the track? I didn't have time to think about it. I had to move.

It was the fastest I'd ever moved. In one wide arc, I swept the remaining vials out of three human's hands so that they smashed on the ground. The silver liquid foamed and bubbled as they howled in annoyance. Not that I had time to acknowledge it. Two of the wolves were heading to the house, probably to help Sophia, while others were fielding attacks from their pack who remained in human form.

I ran towards one. An old man, pinned down by a wolf with thick black fur. Given he looked like the most vulnerable person out here, I sprinted towards him, yanked the wolf off, and threw it hard towards the wooded area.

It skidded across the winter road, limbs buckling as it rolled. Guilt flashed through me as I saw it struggle to stand. Shifters healed fast, right? As long as I didn't cause too much damage, they'd be fine. That was the aim: enough damage to stop them from hurting people, but not so much that they couldn't recover.

The black-furred wolf rolled its shoulders, muscles

twitching. Then it stood up. And lunged again. I pivoted and went for one of the ones that was approaching the house. I grabbed it by the scruff, preparing to throw it away from the door, when the second one went for my arm.

'Crap!' I screamed as pain shot through my forearm. The same forearm that had been dealt the mermaid venom, too. The damn wolf had sunk its teeth all the way through to the bone and was holding on like its life depended on it. As tears pricked my eyes, I kneed it in the gut. It whimpered at the impact, causing it to let go of my arm, at which point I struck again. My second kick sent it flying across into one of its buddies. As I stared at my arm and the puncture wounds, a series of low growls diverted my attention.

The wolves weren't focused on the rest of the humans anymore or on getting to Ines. They were focused on me.

Great.

'Anyone feel like stepping in and giving me a hand?' I yelled aloud. 'Except you, Pongo. You're off duty. Stay!'

Pongo gave a sharp bark from inside the house, which offered just a modicum of comfort as the wolves bared their teeth.

'You really don't want to do this,' I pleaded. 'Please don't do this. I don't want to hurt you. You don't want to hurt me.'

One pounced.

'Okay, you want to hurt me,' I muttered, flipping my

arm up. He flew over my head and crashed into the ground behind me.

It was messy. Ugly. Utterly unprofessional. Silly, really. I'd spent all that time training Fongo. But I needed to work on my own fighting. Relying on instinct and speed was one thing, but if I were ever attacked by someone actually trained, another vampire, or gods forbid, a group of vampires, I'd be absolutely screwed.

I kept going until I had one pinned, hearing the growls and gasps of the crowd around me, followed by the slam of a car door.

'Enough! You stop now!'

The voice rang out, cutting through the fighting like thunder. Relief flooded through me. Raquel. Raquel was half siren. Did her power work on werewolves? The wolves shuffled as if deciding what to do. Then, with a snap of his jaw, the black one lunged for me again.

So that would be a no.

'Evergreen, you alright?' Alex's voice. They were both here.

'Yes. Ish.' Blood was running from the wound in my arm. Given how my body had reacted to the injury from the mermaid's claw, I'd assumed I couldn't bleed, but this cut was proving otherwise. Not that I was going to say that.

'Great. I can kill you later,' he muttered.

In a heartbeat, he was bounding through the air to me in his lion form. One swipe of his paw was all it took to send two of the wolves flying to the side.

'Elodie, catch!' I looked over to Raquel just in time to see her throw something in my direction. Runed cuffs.

I slapped them onto the nearest wolf still circling me. Instantly, they shifted into a small, bruised, human Rumi Hawkins.

'Sophia's in the house!' I shouted, breathless. 'She's the one behind all this. Not Ines. I need to help her. Help Ines.'

'Go. Alex and I have got this.'

The moment I walked over the threshold I spotted Sophia lying there in her wolf form, her chest rising and falling, despite the knife in her side. Pongo raced to me, but the moment of relief was overridden by the sight of Ines on the floor, her breath a gargle, as if her lungs were filling with blood.

Blood that smelt absolutely divine.

CHAPTER
FORTY-TWO

S ince turning into a vampire, I'd only had blood out of a bag or drowned in coffee from Weirdoughs. I never even considered that I could have it from a live being. I'd never considered myself actually wanting blood, but then it had never been presented to me in that manner before. But now that it was... it was all I could think of.

My fangs were tingling. Burning with need as my nostrils were flooded with the sweet, divine scent of fresh blood. No wonder I hated the taste of it out of the bag. This is what it was meant to taste like. Though I would only have a sip. Just a small sip. Then I'd help Ines.

As I moved towards her, my fangs bared, Pongo jumped up at my side.

'Later, boy,' I said, my voice a low hiss. 'Mummy needs to feed.'

I could see the pulse of her blood. The way it was growing weaker and weaker.

Maybe this would help her. Vampire venom had painkilling properties, didn't it? Yes, this would help her. I took another step towards her, only for a pain to strike in my calf. Pongo had sunk his teeth into me.

'What the hell?'

I raised my hand, ready to slap him. But I stopped. What was I doing? I had never hit an animal before, let alone one I loved as much as I loved Pongo. What was I thinking? I turned back to Ines. Pale, dying Ines. And I had been wanting to feed from her. I hadn't been thinking. That was the truth. I had been overcome with bloodlust. Something I'd never thought would happen.

Shame overwhelmed me as I dropped to the ground by her.

'Ines, it's me, Elodie. Can you hear me? You're going to be okay, you're going to be okay. You stopped the others, we're here now. Everything is okay. Everything is okay.'

'Is Sophia... is she okay? I didn't want to kill her. I didn't want to. Is she alright?'

'It's alright,' I said again. How the hell she could be thinking about her sister at this moment was ridiculous. Sophia had tried to kill her, for crying out loud. But I guess that was sisterly love at the extreme.

'Alex is here, Raquel's here. It's going to be okay. We'll get you to Vincent and he'll fix it. He'll make sure you're okay.'

'I don't think he's going to be able to do that.' Her voice cracked as a single tear rolled down her cheek. 'Can you take me over to her? Take me to my sister.'

I glanced over to where Sophia breathed in ragged breaths and noticed the way her feet were bound together. The bolas. The weapon I had believed Ines had used to kill Wren Belkin, and now she had used it on her own sister in a fight for her life, though by the looks of the floor, Ines had knocked wolf Sophia out with one of the taxidermy monstrosities. Turned out they did have a use, after all.

'You need to stay where you are. You're hurt,' I said. The wound on her stomach looked like Sophia had taken a full chunk out of her. With an injury like that, it was a miracle she was alive at all. But then, she was a para. A para who was dying, judging by the way her pulse weakened.

'Please. I want to be with her, Elodie.'

Searing pain continued to throb through my arm, and the entirety of my side was covered in blood, but whatever I was going through, it wasn't a patch on how she was suffering, in every respect. Besides, I would heal soon enough.

'I've got you, I've got you,' I whispered. I lifted her carefully, unable to fight the hiss that escaped me as my arm struck against her side.

'You're hurt,' she said.

'It's fine, it's fine.' I had moved around her, bracing my injured arm against her side when the tingling started.

For a second, I assumed it was body heat. Her blood was warm on my skin, but something about it was different. A static spark was alighting between us. A veil, thrumming with magic.

'Elodie, I didn't think dying would feel like this,' she said softly. 'And it feels nice. It feels... kind of tingly.'

I shifted away from her slightly, still feeling that same gently prickling sensation on my skin. Ines's breathing was lighter now. There was less gargle in her lungs. But it didn't sound like she was slipping away. No, it didn't sound like that at all.

I looked down at her. The puncture wounds where my arm had touched her were healing. Melding together before my very eyes.

'Lie down,' I said quickly, easing her to the ground. Still breathing. Still alive.

'Sophia?' There was desperation in her voice, but I ignored it.

'I'll get to her,' I said instead as I tore open the front of her T-shirt and pressed my injured arms against her stomach.

'Elodie, what are you doing?'

It wasn't Ines who spoke. It was Alex, standing in the doorway, watching me with a pair of runed cuffs in his hand.

'I think... I don't know,' I said. Blood from my arm was dripping freely. The tingling surged through me again. Ines's breathing steadied. 'I think it's healing her.'

'The pain... the pain's leaving,' Ines's throat crackled as tears filled her eyes. 'I can, I can breathe.'

'Stay still,' I said, placing my hand on her shoulder,

trying to stop her from moving, though she was having none of it.

'I'm okay. I'm...I'm okay.'

Despite me trying to get her to stay where she was, she pushed herself to sitting and stared at the place on her stomach where her largest wound had been.

'What happened?' Alex said, wide-eyed and staring.

I didn't reply. I didn't know how. The tingling in my arm continued, but it felt secondary to everything else. Something big had happened. Too big for me to make sense of. In the end, though, it was Ines who spoke, though she too struggled, to find the words.

'I think,' her eyes locked on mine. 'I think Elodie just healed me with her blood.'

FORTY-THREE

Even Sophia's ragged breaths and the shouting that filtered in from outside couldn't obscure the silence that filled the space between Ines, Alex, and me. Ines was sitting completely upright now, her breathing steady, her heartbeat strong.

'I didn't know vampire blood could do that,' Alex whispered quietly. 'Elodie, are you—?' I didn't know how he was going to finish that sentence, but I stopped him before he could get any more words out.

'I'm fine. Sophia's fine. We need to help Raquel. Stop the wolves outside,' I went to move, but Alex grabbed hold of my hand, drawing my eyes to him. 'Raquel's sorted it. They're cuffed in the police car. Well, those of them that could fit in there. The rest are sitting outside it.' His face remained crinkled with concern as he spoke, while never once losing my gaze. 'Are you okay?'

'I'm, I'm...Pongo?' I said, sudden panic soaring

through me. 'Where's Pongo? Pongo!' At the sound of his name, Pongo's head appeared from behind the sofa. Then, after seeing the coast was clear, he ran over to me. With a sigh of relief, I buried my head in his fur, the tingly sensation in my arm all but gone.

'Is Sophia unconscious?' Alex said to Ines while I continued to fuss over my dog. I wasn't sure who needed the hugs more, him or me.

'Yeah,' Ines said. 'She's going to need help, though. I stabbed her in the legs. To slow her down, you know. I think I missed everything important, though. I hope I did.' The way she said it, like she was worried we would judge her for injuring her sister, made my heart ache. I thought it was a miracle she hadn't killed her. Clearly Sophia hadn't shown the same sort of restraint.

'I'll get these on her before she comes around,' Alex said, lifting the cuffs as he walked towards the wolf's body.

'I should leave,' I said, moving to stand up. 'Nyrah needs to know it was tree sprite magic used to make the hex. She should be able to lift it then.' I would need to tell Bobby too, obviously. We would have to work out how we were going to present the story. Or *stories*. There were definitely a few articles in the making. I might not have been on the island long, but even I knew the wolves changing at will was big news. Big news that could cause a lot of fear and worry if not handled properly. And then there was the fact that Sophia had worked with sprites to make hexes. That seemed like a headline-worthy piece in itself, but I'd probably have to check with Diego how to best go about it without undermining Ines's position in the pack.

Wanting to keep Pongo close, I scooped him up in my arms, before pushing myself onto my feet. I had barely taken a step when Ines grabbed me by the shoulder.

'Thank you,' she said, her eyes glazed as they stared into mine. 'Whatever you did, however you did it.'

Dryness filled my throat as I glanced down at my arm. Even though most of it was lost in Pongo's fur, I could already feel the wound was healing, if not gone altogether. There was certainly no pain.

'Yes, about that,' I said, swallowing as I tried to find the words. 'It was probably some werewolf thing.'

Ines's lips pursed. 'I've been around a lot of injured werewolves in my life, both in human and wolf form, and I can promise you, that was nothing to do with us.'

'You guys okay if I do this?' Alex asked, pointing at the cuffs. 'It might bring her around, and, well... you know.'

I knew exactly what he was saying; he didn't want Sophia listening into our conversation. Whatever had happened when I'd helped Ines, it was not up for public debate. My love for Alex grew a little bit more in that moment. Possibly even more so than when he'd stopped me from being ripped to shreds by a group of angry werewolves.

I nodded. 'Yeah, it's fine. You can cuff her,' I said.

A moment later, a perfectly human but utterly unconscious Sophia was on the floor. The knives Ines had thrown were still protruding from her legs and the bolas still wrapped tight around her ankles.

'We should probably get her to Vincent,' Alex said.

'You can take your time,' Ines said, offering Sophia the first glare I'd seen since she challenged her. 'As long as she's alright, that is. A bit of pain might make her think about what she's done.'

I wasn't going to disagree. Sophia deserved to be punished for what she'd put Ines through, not to mention Diego and Theodora.

'You got her?' I asked.

'Sure,' Alex nodded, crouched down, and hoisted Sophia into his arms as if she was weightless. With Pongo still in my arms, I watched him leave, but rather than following, I turned to Ines. Once again, guilt for having assumed she was responsible flowed through me.

'I'm so sorry' I said. 'I'm so sorry that I thought it was you.'

She shook her head and let out a strained laugh. 'Don't be ridiculous. I'd be dead if it wasn't for you. I'm just sorry I didn't know what Sophia was doing. I should have known.'

'You can't know what every member of your pack is up to,' I said, seeing the way her own guilt weighed heavily on her.

'Dad trusts me to do exactly that while he's away. And I let him down. And if you hadn't...you hadn't.' She shook the words away, and with it freed several stray tears that trickled down her cheeks. 'I—I won't say a thing,' she whispered. 'Ever. I promise you. You saved me, Elodie. And I will take the secret to the grave, if that's what you need me to do.'

'Thank you,' I said, not sure what other comment I could give. 'Take care, Ines. I'll see you around.'

She nodded, wiping her cheeks. 'I'd like that. I'd like that very much.'

FORTY-FOUR

Outside, Alex was standing over Rumi Hawkins and another werewolf, who were both sitting on the ground in runed cuffs and looking very sorry for themselves. Their heads were hung low, and from the angle which Rumi was clutching his wrist I assumed it was broken, but I didn't feel even the briefest glimmer of sympathy. I didn't know which one of them had bitten me, or if it even was one of them, but a couple of black eyes and broken bones that would heal far faster than the average human seemed the least they deserved for everything they had done.

As he saw me coming, Alex muttered something to the two wolves before walking over to me.

'How are you doing, Evergreen?' he asked.

'I'm okay,' I said, only to change my mind. 'I nearly fed from her, Alex.'

'You did?' his jaw fell open, before he closed it again, and shook his head. 'Shit.'

'I don't know what came over me.' My voice was barely a whisper. 'It was like I wasn't in control. If Pongo hadn't been there, I...I don't know what would have happened.'

'It wasn't on you,' he said, placing a hand on my arm. 'Werewolf blood's toxic to vampires. Designed to draw you in and poison you. You did good Elodie. Fighting that and then, well whatever you did after, you did good. Believe me.'

Tears stung my eyes. 'I should get back. I'm okay now. Honestly. I'm okay.'

'Sure.' His eyes were locked on mine, like he didn't really believe I was okay at all, but then, that was probably fair enough. 'I'm okay,' was like 'I'm fine,' words people said when they didn't have enough strength to say the truth, or didn't feel like anyone actually wanted to hear it. For me, it was the former. I didn't doubt that Alex would understand whatever I told him, but for the moment, I couldn't get any more words out.

'I've got to sit here and wait for Raquel to come back with a squad car. Though she's got to get the other wolves secured in cells first and get someone in to watch them,' Alex said. 'But I was thinking, those two can't do anything with the cuffs on them. We can squeeze them and us back into your Mini and take them to the station. Might be a bit quicker?'

I looked at the men. Rumi might have been a small, gangly teenager, but that didn't change how they would be cramped in the back of my car, that was for sure. And did I really want to be in a small enclosed space with two of the people who'd just attacked me?

'Maybe you're better off waiting,' I said.

'Right.' Alex pursed his lips. 'Only I'd really prefer to get them back as quick as possible, though. You know, give Raquel a hand?'

I didn't want to, but he had come to my rescue in a big way. I didn't want to leave him standing here for hours, either.

'Fine,' I said, pulling my keys out of my pocket only to stop. I hadn't realised my hands were trembling, but the keys were practically jangling. And now that I was aware of it, they weren't the only part of my body that was moving by themselves. My knees had a definite quake to them and noticing it only seemed to make them worse.

'I'll drive,' Alex said, taking the keys from me, his eyes meeting mine with the slightest glint in them.

'It wasn't about getting them back quickly at all, was it?' A flutter of gratitude wafted through me.

'I don't know what you're on about,' he said, a smile tugging at his lips as he turned around and walked back to the wolves.

BY THE TIME we arrived at the hospital, Bobby, Chloe and Dylan were there, filling the tiny waiting area.

'Nyrah's working on undoing the hexes now,' Chloe said when she finally released my hug. 'I still can't believe it. Sprites working with wolves. Teaching them magic. I thought they hated each other.'

'Maybe that's just a sign of how bad things have got in the forest,' I suggested.

They nodded in agreement.

'We need to have a serious talk about you following leads on your own.' Bobby's voice was the firmest I'd ever heard. If we'd been in the office, this would feel like an official warning. 'I don't know how your London paper worked, but a scoop is not worth your life. You understand me?'

'In my defence, I didn't know I'd be dealing with werewolves in wolf form.'

His eyebrow rose so high it jiggled his eye patch. 'But you went into a werewolf pack, believing its beta had already harmed two of your colleagues?' He had me there. I pressed my lips together, but before I could say any more, he engulfed me in his giant-like body and pulled me into him. The first time I had met Bobby I had felt this paternal vibe radiating from him, and in the absence of my actual dad hugging me at that moment, he was definitely the next best thing.

'Any chance you can let her go so someone else can get a turn, Bobby?' I broke away from Bobby to find Whip standing there. His face pale. 'Please tell me that Raquel was exaggerating when she said she found you battling four werewolves by yourself.'

As he walked towards me, I felt the others drop away.

'I could tell you that,' I said, 'if that's what you'd like to hear.'

With a long sigh, he sidled up next to me and dropped his head onto my shoulder. I'd never noticed how deeply he smelt of the sea. As if he belonged to it. Which, I guess, in some ways, he did.

'You are going to be the death of me, you know that?'

'I'm alright, you know,' I said, lifting his head up so he could look me in the eye. 'Honestly, when Alex showed up, he took most of them out.'

Whip placed his hand on my cheek and brushed a strand of hair behind my ear.

'I don't understand how you do it,' he said.

'How I get myself into so much trouble?' I questioned, quirking my lips. 'It's pretty easy, really. I just listen to the good advice people give me and actively ignore it.'

He let out a deep chuckle that caused his dimple to flicker into life.

'Not what I meant. No, I mean how you've got me so hooked.'

He moved his hand from my cheek and brushed it against my bottom lip.

'What happened to remaining professional in a work environment?' I whispered, annoyingly aware of how breathy my voice sounded.

'Let's just call this extenuating circumstances,' he said, before planting his lips against mine.

Like every kiss I shared with Whip, it was phenomenal, but it was also tender. Soft. Intimate, especially considering the surroundings and when I broke away, I stared deep into those peridot eyes.

'Now that I've got you here,' I said, offering him my most sultry voice. 'Any chance you want to give a quote? You know, for The Oracle?'

He chuckled again as he brushed another strand of hair behind my ear. 'My quote would be that since Elodie Evergreen turned up in Ravens Hollow, my life's been turned upside down in ways I couldn't have ever imagined.'

'I don't think that's the type of thing the readers would want.'

With a deep laugh, he wrapped me in his arms and pulled me into him.

'You know, I still haven't got Nyrah to do that extra ward on your house. And she's going to be pretty busy tonight, working on the antidote with Vincent.'

'So what do you suggest?' I asked.

'You probably shouldn't sleep on your own, and I would offer to sleep on your sofa again, but it's not that comfortable, if I'm honest.'

I laughed, 'I'm sure we'll figure something out,' I said, before planting my lips on his and kissing him. A massive scoop, and a man I was pretty sure I could now call my boyfriend. It had been one heck of a day, that was for sure.

FORTY-FIVE

The next morning, when I woke up, I ached. Really ached. Legs, arms, my abs. No muscles had been spared. It felt as if I had gone three rounds in a boxing ring against a seasoned professional. Which was, essentially what I had done.

With a low groan, I rolled over, to find the other half of my bed occupied, although it was with a substantially less furry occupant than usual.

Fully dressed, other than shoes and socks, Whip lay with his head next to mine, a smile on his lips.

'Morning,' he whispered.

'Morning.'

We had talked all night, about lots and nothing. I told him about growing up, about the way my mum, Maria, had disappeared when I was so young and how close Dad and I were, but how I'd struggled to see him as much as I should have with work. He told me pieces of how he'd lost his family, too. Only in a very different way. As sirens, his family had aged slowly, but they had still aged. Grown old while he'd been cursed to immortality. To watch them fade and die one by one. Which, he explained, was probably why he'd formed such a close bond with his stepsister, a vampire who had been cursed by the same person who had cursed him.

'I'm definitely going to have to learn to fight,' I groaned stretching out my neck and arms hoping it would alleviate some of the tenderness. It didn't. 'I'm stiff as hell.'

'Or you could just stay out of trouble,' Whip suggested.

'Now that doesn't sound anywhere near as much fun,' I grinned. It didn't seem real that this beautiful not-quite-human was there, sharing my bed. Not that he had even been below the blanket, but one of the things we had spoken about was taking things slowly, and after the way life had been in Ravens Hollow since I moved, slowly felt good. Still, I leaned in, ready for my first kiss of the day, when a sound reverberated from the living room.

Food. Food. Walk. Food. Elodie. Food. A moment later, Pongo appeared at the foot of the bed, before bounding up and landing on my very tender stomach. He had fallen sleep by my feet and I couldn't help but feel the noisy, bouncing waking up was punishment for being relegated from his normal pillow position.

'I guess that's my cue to get up,' I chuckled and shifted over, so that Pongo fell into the centre of the bed between us. 'Fancy walking me to work?'

'Absolutely.'

As much as I loved driving my Maureen around the island, I actually loved walking hand in hand with Whip, even more. Andy had never been a hand holder. Or a kisser. Or any form of affection giver, really. Although Pongo didn't make it particularly easy. Likely still annoyed by the bed situation, he continually put himself between us. Thankfully, he was still little enough that Whip and I could hold hands, anyway. When we reached the paper, he stopped and kissed me slowly. I was so lost in the moment that it was only when there was a clearing of the throat behind me that I realised there were other people around.

'Well, this is new. How long have I been out of it, exactly?'

My heart leapt in my chest. I spun around at the voice.

'Diego!' I moved from Whip and immediately swung my arms around my colleague. Never had calloused skin felt so good against my body. Pink, humanish, calloused skin. 'You're okay. Thank God you're okay.'

'I am. Theodora's already up there. She got out of it faster than me.' He shook his head. 'Werewolves. I can't believe it. They're an embarrassment to our type. That damn pack.'

'It wasn't that pack's fault at all,' I said. 'Ines did what she could. It's not like she's the Alpha, is it? Why the hell wasn't he there?'

Whip and Diego exchanged a look, which I tried to read. 'I guess there's a story there,' I said. 'You'll have to fill me in later. First, we need some celebratory treats. What do you fancy? Doughnuts? Banana cake?'

'I'm good with anything,' Diego replied. 'Well... anything other than mango hooch.'

I SAT BACK in my seat and looked at the first draft of my new story. The headline, *The Wolf and the Wood Sprites*, was written in bold across the screen. It was a good first draft, but I wanted to get a few more details, quotes from Ines and such, but I figured I should give her a little time to recover. There was so much to write about I was going to get at least another couple of stories out of it. Meaning there was no rush to see her now.

'Hey Evergreen, how are you doing?'

I swivelled around on my chair to find Alex standing there, trademark grin on his lips. He was wearing his standard short-sleeved uniform, though for once, my eyes weren't drawn to the tightness around his biceps. It was his forearms, covered in cuts and bruises, that held my attention. I'd been in so much shock the day before, I hadn't even noticed that he'd been hurt, too.

'Oh my god,' I said, standing up. 'Are you okay? I didn't realise you were injured.'

'It's nothing, honestly,' he said. 'A couple of decent shifts and it'll all be healed. I'm planning on going for a run this afternoon, actually, but I wondered if this morning you wanted to see if we could track down that sireless vamp. Unless you need some more time to rest, that is. Desk duty and all that?' His eyes glinted, like he already knew my answer.

I recalled Whip's earlier comment about staying out of trouble. But this wasn't dangerous. I was going to speak to another vampire, that was all. And I'd have Pongo and Alex with me.

'Let me get Pongo's leash,' I said.

We left the office in silence, a flurry of unspoken words filling the space between us.

'Have you told Whip yet?' Alex said, eventually. 'You know, about what happened yesterday with Ines?'

I shook my head. 'No... not yet. I'm not exactly sure how to.' I had thought about it countless time over the night. After all, all we'd been doing was talking. But Whip'd been so relieved that I hadn't been seriously hurt, I didn't want to tell him about the bite. I tried to segue in without specifics, though. About different creatures and their healing abilities. Witches and fairies, yes. Selkies too, with their pelts, though that was a one-off, but at no point did he mention vampires.

'I get it, I do,' Alex said. 'But from a practical point of view, he's old. I'm pretty sure he's one of the oldest people on the island. He knows a lot of things. Might be helpful.'

Whip was one of the oldest people on the island. What the hell? I brushed the thought from my mind. I knew he was immortal. So was I. It was just something I'd have to wrap my head around. The sea had just come into view when Alex stopped and turned to face me. For some reason, Pongo didn't mind Alex and me walking next to each other, but that was probably because I'd given him enough snacks that he was over his sulk.

'I won't tell anyone, you know,' Alex said, locking his eye on mine. 'Whatever you are, whatever happened. I should have said that yesterday, but I won't tell anyone.'

'I know,' I said. Ines had said the same to me, and I had been grateful for her assurance, but strange, as it was, I'd never even questioned whether Alex would let Raquel or anyone else know. We were friends, and he was the type of person who protected the people he cared about. I already knew that.

'Can I ask you something?' he said. 'Something about you and Whip.'

'Sure, I guess. How awkward is it going to be?'

'Probably no more awkward than things are right now,' he said with a chuckle. I couldn't help but reciprocate. It went a little way to easing some of the tension around us.

Alex blew out a deep breath. 'I like him, I do. I know he's a good guy.'

'That doesn't sound like much of a question.'

'No, you're right. And you can tell me to butt out, but

when he was gone at the organised crime conference, did he ask you anything?'

'Like what?'

'I dunno. To wait for him? To not start seeing anyone else while he was gone, maybe?'

So much for not getting more awkward.

'Well, we kind of hoped we'd get to go on a date or something first. It didn't happen. So he asked me if we could do it when he got back.'

Alex's Adam's apple bobbed visibly as he swallowed. Clearly, this conversation wasn't coming easy for him. And I still wasn't entirely sure what point he was trying to make.

'I get it, I do,' he said as he started walking again. 'It's just... should he have had to ask?'

'What do you mean?' A surge of anger flurried through my body. 'Are you saying you think he used his powers, because I can tell you right now—'

'No, no, that's not what I meant at all,' Alex hurriedly tried to retract his words, though my anger continued to thrum within me. 'I just mean that if you and him were meant to be, then it would've been a given, right? And if he needed to ask, well, then, was it because he was trying to keep you from seeing if there was anyone else there, that maybe you were a better fit with?'

A better fit. He was meaning him, right? Silence bloomed.

'Alex...' I started, not sure how I was going to continue... 'You're a good friend but—'

He shook his head and laughed in a way that caused me to stop.

'That's not what I'm saying, Elodie. I'm not. It might sound like that, and yes, I think you're great, but there are a lot of great people on this island, and beyond it, for that matter. I'm speaking as your friend. That's it. You were engaged right, to a complete douche?'

'That's one way of putting it.'

'And now, you arrive here, and you're immediately in a relationship with a guy I'm pretty sure you've not been on a date with. You've not been on a date with anyone, I don't think. You barely know what it's like to be a para, let alone part of the world.' He let out a long breath. 'I guess what I'm saying is take things slow, okay? You've been through enough. I don't want to see you hurt.'

I wasn't sure how to reply, so I didn't. His heartbeat was strong and steady. He was telling me the truth. On some level, anyway. He was a friend, trying to protect me. But I was also a grown woman. My throat cracked as I tried to decide whether I wanted to thank him, or tell him to mind his own business, when he spoke again.

'This is us,' he said. 'We're here.'

We were standing in a small square outside the beachside shops, with flats above them where people lived, and though Alex's words lingered in my mind, I refocused on the current situation.

'What did you say the person's name was?' I said.

'Hold on.' Alex flicked up his phone. 'Maria,' he said. 'No surname.'

Maria. My throat tightened. That had been my mother's name. My father had used to sing it constantly, the song from *West Side Story*. Even now, I couldn't hear that song without an uncomfortable twist in my gut.

'And we're sure she's still there?'

'That's the name the property's registered to. I checked the records. There are four other Marias on the island, but they live in packs, so I don't think they're the person. Guess it's time we see.'

My nerves were far higher than I expected them to be as we knocked on the door and waited.

'Looks like we might meet our first other vamp,' I whispered to Pongo, only for a sound from inside to steal my attention. 'I can hear footsteps,' I said. 'Someone's coming.'

We waited, and a moment later, the door swung open. Rather than a vampire standing there, it was a familiar face, with pointed ears tilted at a forty-five degree angle. Someone I had actually suspected once of being involved in the hexes.

'Amira,' I said, surprised by the figure standing in front of me.

'Elodie?' Her voice was bright, although her eyes narrowed as she saw Alex standing beside me. 'How can I help you?'

'Amira, we were actually looking for somebody who may have lived here before you. A vampire called Maria.'

'Maria?' she said. Her eyes widened slightly, and I searched for a hitch in her pulse, only I couldn't hear it. I couldn't hear her pulse at all. I knew that some faes and shifters had heartbeats so fast they were practically a buzz, but none? That didn't feel right.

'Can we come in?' I said, shooting Alex a look that told him to be alert.

Her smile tightened ever so slightly before it settled.

'Of course. Yes. Absolutely.'

We followed her up a steep, narrow staircase. Pongo and I walked behind Amira, as Alex closed the door behind us.

'How long have you lived here, Amira?' I said, as we entered a small living space. It was tidy and clean, other than one mug on the windowsill, yet it lacked homey touches. There was only one photo frame I could see, and it was tilted away from me.

'Oh, twenty years, I think. Give or take.'

'Right,' I said, trying to sound casual. 'And have you been pretending to be a fae all that time?'

Her jaw dropped. As did Alex's.

'Elodie,' he whispered, but I didn't even turn to look at him.

'The mug over there. It's had blood in it, but from the smells in this room, no one else has been in here for days, if not longer. And you've no pulse. Amira. It's an anagram for Maria. You registered as a vampire, then got here and found a way to disguise yourself. So why did you disguise yourself? Was it to hide from whoever sired you?'

Amira didn't speak. Her lips were pressed together.

'You always were so smart,' she said eventually. 'I should have known you'd figure it out.'

The comment caught me by surprise.

'We just want to ask you some questions,' Alex said, breaking the silence before it could settle. 'About being sireless. We were hoping you could share a few details about your turning with us?'

Amira was still looking straight at me, as if she hadn't even heard what Alex had asked her. As if she wasn't even aware he was in the room. Like it was just her and I. Dryness swept through my throat as a tremble gripped my hand. She was waiting for me. Waiting for me to speak. To ask her something. But I didn't. Instead, I walked over to the window and picked up the photo frame.

'Elodie, what is it?' Alex's voice cut through the silence, but I couldn't reply. All my attention had been taken by the item in my hands. It was a family photo, taken on a beach. The background itself was nondescript, really. White sand. Blue skies. It could have been a thousand places on the planet. But it wasn't. I knew exactly where it was. It was the Seychelles. A picture of a family in the Seychelles. It was, in fact, the last family photo they'd ever had and I knew that, because I had the exact same one, shoved in a drawer somewhere back in England. Tears filled my eyes. It couldn't be. It just couldn't be.

'Elodie,' Amira's voice was low and trembling. 'Any chance you could give your mother a hug?'

THIS ELODIE ADVENTURE might be over, but how about a fresh perspective with a bonus chapter?

Send me my exclusive bonus chapter.

DEMONS AND DEALINES
RAVENS HOLLOW INVESTIGATIONS BOOK 3

A family reunion, a deadly scoop, and secrets sharper than my fangs...

Life as a **vampire journalist** was finally settling down. I had my dream job at *The Oracle*, a loyal (if slobbery) pup, and a maybe-relationship that didn't involve murder investigations.

Then my **long-lost mother** crashes back into my life with a revelation that rewrites everything I thought I knew about my family...

Before I can process the truth, another story lands on my desk, pulling me into a dangerous game of **demon bargains**, shifting alliances, and bodies piling up faster than I can chase the leads.

Now it's not just my career on the line; t's my heart, my friends, and possibly every paranormal on the island. But if there's one thing I know.

I'm Elodie Evergreen. **I chase the truth, even when it has claws.**

SCAN ME

Note from Ella

First off, thank you for taking the time to read **Hexes and Headlines**, the second book in the *Ravens Hollow Investigations Series*. If you enjoyed the book, I'd love for you to let your friends know so they can also experience this action-packed adventure. I have enabled the lending feature where possible, so it is easy to share with a friend.

If you leave a review **Hexes and Headlines** on <u>Amazon</u>, Goodreads, Bookbub, or even your own blog or social media, I would love to read it. You can email me the link at <u>ella@ellastoneauthor.com</u>

Don't forget, you can stay up-to-date on upcoming releases and sales by joining my newsletter, following my social media pages or visiting my website www.ellastoneauthor.com

ABOUT ELLA STONE

Lover of all things magical, mysterious, and mildly chaotic, Ella Stone writes fast-paced urban fantasy with a generous pinch of paranormal drama, a splash of slow-burn romance, and enough supernatural shenanigans to keep your heart pounding and your tea cold.

When not plotting vampire betrayals or helping werewolves find some clothes (and occasionally their dignity), she's usually curled up with a book, surrounded by cats who believe they own the place—and, frankly, they do.

Her books include the *Dark Creatures* saga, the *Bloodsucker's Blog* trilogy, the *Witchlight Magical Mysteries* (co-written with the brilliant Heather G. Harris), and the brand new *Ravens Hollow Investigations*—a series full of magical crimes, dangerous alliances, and secrets that refuse to stay buried.

Expect charm, danger, and just enough mayhem to make things interesting. Welcome to her world. It's weird, it's wicked, and you're going to love it here.